"There's something I'd like to ask you...

"That is, if you do decide to stay in Gabriel Bend for a while. I mean, you and Davey seem to hit it off, and obviously he's having a blast with Shadow. When we saw his doctor this afternoon, she said it could help so much if he had a male mentor in his life, so I was wondering…" Running out of words, Holly cast him a pleading look, hoping he'd get the message.

Mark opened his mouth as if to reply before clamping it shut again. He shook his head and glanced away.

"I'm so sorry," she said, wringing her hands. "We hardly know each other, and that was terribly presumptuous of me. Please, forget I asked."

"No…no, it's all right." His whole body seemed to sag, even as a tentative smile returned. "You flatter me, that's all."

Alone on the porch with Mark, she bit her lower lip. "So…would you maybe think about mentoring Davey? For his sake?" *And for mine?*

Award-winning author **Myra Johnson** writes emotionally gripping stories about love, life and faith. She is a two-time finalist for the ACFW Carol Award and winner of the 2005 RWA Golden Heart® Award. Married since 1972, Myra and her husband have two married daughters and seven grandchildren. She and her husband reside in Texas, sharing their home with two pampered rescue dogs.

Books by Myra Johnson

Love Inspired

The Ranchers of Gabriel Bend

The Rancher's Family Secret
The Rebel's Return
The Rancher's Family Legacy

Rancher for the Holidays
Her Hill Country Cowboy
Hill Country Reunion
The Rancher's Redemption
Their Christmas Prayer

Visit the Author Profile page at LoveInspired.com.

The Rancher's
Family Legacy

Myra Johnson

LOVE INSPIRED
INSPIRATIONAL ROMANCE

LOVE INSPIRED®
INSPIRATIONAL ROMANCE

ISBN-13: 978-1-335-75930-6

The Rancher's Family Legacy

Copyright © 2022 by Myra Johnson

For questions and comments about the quality of this book, please contact us at CustomerService@Harlequin.com.

Love Inspired
22 Adelaide St. West, 41st Floor
Toronto, Ontario M5H 4E3, Canada
www.LoveInspired.com

Printed in U.S.A.

Recycling programs
for this product may
not exist in your area.

This is the day which the Lord hath made;
we will rejoice and be glad in it.
—*Psalm* 118:24

In memory of Shadow, a very special rescue dog, though I'm not sure who rescued whom.
I still miss you, sweet boy!

Chapter One

"Shadow, fetch!"

The furry black mutt, about the size of a border collie and twice as smart, darted after the tennis ball. Mark Caldwell laughed as the dog raced back to drop the slobbery ball into his outstretched hand. "Good boy."

Kneeling to give Shadow a thorough scratching behind the ears, Mark took in the early-November fall vistas of the Texas Hill Country northwest of Austin. Though no match for Mark's home state of Montana, the scenery here at the quarter horse ranch his grandfather Arturo Navarro had established over sixty years ago claimed its own kind of rugged beauty. For Mark's uncle Hank and twin cousins, Spencer and Samuel, the ranch was home, but until April, when Mark had flown in from Montana with his parents for his grandfather's ninetieth birthday, he hadn't visited more than a handful of times.

Now, only seven months later, here he was again, this time for his grandfather's memorial service, held yesterday at the family's church in Gabriel Bend. Mom and Dad had opted to fly again, but Mark disliked having to crowbar his brawny, long-legged frame into a cramped airline seat, so he'd left a few days ahead of his parents to drive down in his much roomier Chevy Silverado truck.

After the reading of the will this morning, Mark almost wished he'd stayed home, because Tito—short for the Spanish *abuelito*, "grandpa"—couldn't have been thinking straight when he'd specified the terms for dividing his estate. As expected, Uncle Hank inherited half the ranch, and it had seemed only right that the other half would go to Mark's mother, Alicia. Not that Mom had any interest in owning a share of the ranch, but she was certainly entitled to its value if Hank wanted to buy her out.

Instead, to everyone's surprise, Tito had designated the other half to be equally divided three ways—a third each to Spencer and Samuel, and the remaining third to Mark, *but* with the stipulation that he must commit to living and working at the ranch for one year.

This was beyond absurd. What did he know about horses or ranching? Besides, his whole life was back in Missoula. His home, his construction company…

His memories.

He shifted his thoughts to Tito's only bequest to Mark's mother—a decrepit old cabin on one puny half acre at the southwest edge of the ranch near the river. Mom and Tito had never been close, but *seriously*?

Shadow yipped and pranced, begging him to toss the ball.

"Okay, okay." Still preoccupied after hiking out for a look at the cabin, he gave the ball a hard throw.

A couple dozen yards ahead, the ball ricocheted off a rock in the lane and bounced over a wire mesh pasture fence. Shadow headed for a nearby gate and ducked beneath the bottom rail, then ran in circles looking to see where it had landed.

"Can't find it, boy?" Mark jogged to the fence and scanned the area beyond. No sign of a grungy yellow tennis ball.

Continuing the search, the dog expanded his range to where a sprawling live oak supported a dilapidated old tree house. He halted abruptly, his attention captured by a tawny-haired boy, maybe nine or ten years old, crouched on the rotting boards.

A boy Mark suspected had no business exploring on Navarro land.

"Hey, kid." He tried not to sound scary as he slipped through the gate and ambled over. "You live around here?"

"N-no. I was just, um…" With Shadow parked at the base of the tree, the boy didn't look too certain about climbing down.

"It's okay, he won't hurt you. Shadow loves kids." Or maybe it was Mark who intimidated the boy. Attempting to appear less threatening, he squatted next to Shadow.

Almost at once, the dog's demeanor changed. A low whine emanated from Shadow's throat. His front paws tapped the ground in a nervous rhythm, his gaze fixed on the boy. As his whining grew increasingly urgent, the kid began trembling. A second later, he toppled from the ledge.

On pure instinct, Mark lunged to break the boy's fall, catching him in time to keep his head from slamming into the hard ground. This was no tree-climbing accident—the kid was in the throes of a seizure. Not that Mark was any expert, but he knew enough to roll the boy onto his side and make sure he couldn't hurt himself on anything. Quiet now, Shadow lay close in the protective posture he'd always displayed with Kellie.

The memory—and the latent grief it churned up—caught Mark off guard. Three years now, and he still hadn't gotten over losing his daughter. He choked down a swallow and focused his attention on the boy.

The episode was mild and short-lived, and after several minutes of recovery, the kid opened his eyes. "Where—what—" He groaned.

"You had a seizure. Are you feeling okay?"

The boy gave a wobbly nod. "Aw, Mom's gonna be so mad at me."

"I'm sure she'll be glad you're all right. Has this happened before?"

"Yeah, sometimes. I take medicine, but it doesn't always work."

"Wow, that's rough." Mark slid an arm under the boy's shoulder. "Can you sit up?"

He blinked a few times, looking dazed, then flinched when he noticed Shadow next to him.

"Don't be scared. He's been watching over you till you felt better. What's your name?"

"Davey."

"Hi, Davey. That's my dad's name, too. Well, actually, David." Hopefully his chatter would help put the boy at ease. "This is my dog, Shadow. I'm Mark."

Sitting up slowly, Davey tentatively patted Shadow on the head. "Nice doggy."

"So where is your mom?" Mark pulled his cell phone from his jeans pocket. "Give me her number and I'll call her for you."

"No, please, she'll just worry." Davey scrambled to his feet, then wavered.

"As well she should." Mark pushed up from the

ground and steadied the boy. "Look, you're not a hundred percent yet. Let me drive you home. My truck's—"

"That's okay. Mom's right next door."

"Right next..." Scrunching a brow, he looked across the pastures. "At the McClement ranch?"

"Yeah, she works there. With Aunt Jo-Jo and Aunt Lindsey."

Mark's cousins' wives. The three best friends ran River Bend Events and Wedding Chapel on the ranch owned by Lindsey and her aunt, Audra Forrester. Mark couldn't recall meeting Davey's mother, but he must have, since she'd handled the catering for his grandfather's big birthday bash last spring. That had been an evening to remember in more ways than one—barely more so than today's reading of the will.

"Well, we'd better get you over there. Your mom needs to know about the seizure." And be reminded not to let a kid with a serious disorder like this go wandering across a working horse ranch. "Want to ride in my truck, or do you feel up to walking?"

"I can walk. I know a shortcut." Looking nervous and not at all steady on his feet, Davey backed away. "And you don't have to go with me. I'm fine now. Promise."

Mark got the sense the kid was less afraid of being escorted home by a stranger than of how his mother would react to learning he'd had a seizure—or possibly *where* he'd had the seizure. "You're still pretty shaky. I'd feel a lot better if I go along to be sure you make it okay. Now, where's this shortcut?"

Giving a huff, Davey grudgingly led him down the lane. Past the main barn, they crossed a paddock behind a smaller barn and came out at an opening in the barbed-wire fence that separated the Navarro and McClement properties. Hidden by twisted cedars and brushy undergrowth, a section of barbed wire had been propped open with old tree branches. Mark vaguely remembered it from his rare childhood visits to the ranch.

The kid scooted through the gap, then looked back as if hoping Mark wouldn't follow. It would be a tight squeeze, but he didn't intend to let Davey out of his sight until the boy was safely back in his mother's care.

In the meantime, Shadow hopped through and scampered over, blocking Davey from a quick getaway. Good—Mark and Shadow were on the same page here. He ducked low, hoping not to snag his jacket or jeans. With a grunt, he straightened on the other side and followed a slump-shouldered Davey across the field.

Mark's cousin Spencer, the Navarro twin who'd married Lindsey McClement, was just exiting the barn, where he stabled the rescue horses he fostered. "Hey, Mark." He cast him a concerned smile. "You doing okay?"

Obviously a reference to the terms of the will. "A lot to take in." He gently but firmly clamped his hand on the boy's shoulder in case he got any ideas about escaping. "Is Davey's mom around?"

"They're all in the study discussing what to do about the new event venue building. They just got word their contractor had a family emergency and has to back out." Spencer walked with them to the back porch. "Why are you with Davey? Is there a problem?"

"Best if I just talk to his mom."

With a muttered *uh-oh*, Spencer led Mark and Davey to the study, where the three women were huddled around construction drawings spread across a worktable. Under different circumstances, Mark, a building contractor himself, would have liked a closer look at the plans.

Instead, he took a moment to identify which of the women was Davey's mother. Of course he knew Spencer's wife, the dark-haired Lindsey. Joella, the sophisticated blonde, had married Samuel, Spencer's twin, last summer.

The third woman, a little shorter than the other two, had to be the kid's mom. She looked up with a start, her shoulder-length brown waves falling across one eye in a way that made Mark's stomach flutter.

He abruptly tamped down the sensation. This was no time to go soft.

She did look familiar, now that he thought about it. What was her name—Molly? Sally? Something like that.

"Davey?" She shoved a strand of hair behind her ear as her gaze shifted to Mark, and then to the dog at his side. "What's going on?"

Mark nudged the boy. "Are you going to tell your mother, or should I?"

"Tell me what? And I'll thank you to take your hands off my son." Rising, she grabbed Davey's arm and tugged him out of Mark's reach.

Spencer edged between them. "Holly, you remember my cousin Mark Caldwell from Montana?"

Holly—right. She looked about as prickly as the shrub of the same name, and the spark in her flashing green eyes could light a forest fire. "Of course," she said with a dismissive wave. "I— I'm sorry about the loss of your grandfather."

"Thank you." Neither her sympathy nor her attractiveness would deflect him from his purpose. "Can I talk to you privately, please?"

Her brows shot up. "Why? Did Davey do something?"

"Mo-om." The boy exhaled tiredly as he sank into a chair. The poor kid looked wrung out. "I had a seizure. It's no big deal."

"What?" She gripped his upper arms and bent forward until they were eye to eye. "Davey, are you okay? When did it happen? *Where* did it happen?"

"Stop, Mom." The boy's face reddened. Arms locked across his chest, he shrugged off her hold. "I'm not a baby."

So the kid had an independent streak. Even more reason for his mother to keep a closer eye on him. "I found him in one of my uncle's pastures," Mark stated. "He was climbing around in a rotting tree house."

"Oh, Davey." Eyes closed, Holly pressed her lips together and took three slow breaths through her nose. Opening her eyes, she frowned at Mark. "Perhaps we *should* speak privately." To Lindsey, she said, "Can Davey rest in your room for a while?"

"Sure. Come with me, fella." Lindsey escorted the boy down the hall.

Mark and Holly followed but detoured into the living room. Only after she halted and faced him did he realize Shadow had continued on with Davey and Lindsey. Interesting…

Arms folded, the boy's mom tapped her index fingers on the opposite elbows. "So. What exactly happened?"

"Like I said, I found him in one of my uncle's pastures. Rather, my dog found him." He described catching Davey as he fell from the tree house. "He shouldn't have been out there by himself. If there'd been horses in the pasture—or if Shadow and I hadn't happened on him when we did—things could have turned out a lot worse."

Something verging on panic flashed behind those

incredible green eyes before they darkened like storm clouds. "Are you implying I'm a neglectful parent?"

"I'm not *implying* anything, Mrs...."

"Elliot," she supplied, her voice rising. "And it certainly sounds like you are, so why don't you come right out and say it?"

"Fine. I think it's irresponsible of you to let a kid with a seizure disorder go roaming alone where it isn't safe."

"So I'm neglectful *and* irresponsible?"

"I didn't mean—"

Jaw trembling, she motioned toward the front door. "Goodbye, Mr. Caldwell. Thank you for walking Davey back, but you needn't concern yourself any further with my son's well-being."

"Fine by me." This encounter had gotten way out of hand. Probably his fault for speaking his mind, but she needed to hear it. He took three steps toward the door, then remembered Shadow. "My dog—"

Holly glanced around. "Oh. I—I think he must be in the bedroom with Davey."

"If you don't mind, I'd like to fetch him and be on my way." And the sooner, the better.

Shaken by a disconcerting mix of fear, relief and indignation, Holly showed the imposing dark-haired man down the hall so he could get his pet—who didn't appear nearly as anxious to leave as his owner. The shaggy black dog rested his chin on the mattress while Davey sleepily stroked his head.

A shuddering sigh sounded from Mark's chest. Glancing up, she glimpsed a subtle change in his expression. He almost looked...sad. "Shadow," he called roughly, "let's go."

Patting his thigh, he uttered the quiet command twice

more before the dog obeyed. Holly wasn't sure if dogs could actually roll their eyes in annoyance, but it seemed like Shadow did exactly that as he trudged after Mark down the hall.

The dog might be endearing and certainly seemed to have bonded with Davey, but rugged good looks aside, Mark Caldwell was another story. How dare the man accuse her of neglect? He must have no idea how hard it was to be the parent of a child with health issues, or the fine line she walked between protecting Davey and giving him the freedom to be a normal, active little boy.

Still, if she'd had any idea her son had gone exploring on the Navarro ranch—how many times had she warned him to stay close to the house and not to play near the livestock? The McClement cattle ranch held enticements galore for a boy Davey's age. Add Navarro Quarter Horses right next door, and it meant twice the opportunities for getting into dangerous situations.

The thump of boots and click of dog toenails faded as Mark exited through the kitchen. After another deep breath, Holly rejoined her friends in the study.

Joella looked up with concern. "How's Davey?"

"He's resting. Thanks for getting him settled, Lindsey." Suddenly exhausted herself, Holly collapsed into a chair at the worktable. "Okay, where were we?"

"Without a contractor." Joella massaged her temples. "We could sue for breach of contract—Samuel and I are in the same boat, since Jay Graham was building our house. Or we can just be gracious about it and let him go."

Lips pursed, Lindsey nodded. "I think that's our only choice. Jay's a respected member of the community. He's only trying to take care of his family."

"I agree." Holly drummed her fingers on the unfurled

building specs. Incredible that after only a few months in business, River Bend Events and Wedding Chapel was doing well enough to qualify for a loan and permits to erect a permanent structure. The climate-controlled building would enable them to host events all year long, even in inclement weather. As funds permitted, they planned to gradually increase their inventory of equipment and furnishings, offsetting the expense by what they'd save in rental fees.

Except now all those plans were on hold. Shoulders caving, Holly asked, "So what do we do next?"

After a sip of coffee, Joella perused a page in her notebook. "Jay recommended a couple of other local contractors who might be able to take over. What it comes down to is their availability."

Holly pictured the foundation sitting untouched for weeks or possibly months. "Well, we'd better start making calls…"

"I wish we could ask Mark," Lindsey murmured. "Spencer says he's a top-notch building contractor. If nothing else, maybe he could give us some advice."

"Good idea—we should ask." Joella gnawed her lower lip as she stared into her coffee mug. "It sure would be nice if he decided to stay."

Holly looked at her in confusion. "What are you talking about?"

"Arturo's will." Lindsey described how the estate had been divided, including what would be required of Mark to inherit his third of the grandsons' share. "He definitely has some serious thinking to do."

Holly's jaw dropped. "Is he considering staying at the ranch?"

"Samuel's gut feeling is no," Joella said. "Mark's

hoping to meet with the attorney on Monday to discuss his options."

Davey appeared in the doorway. "I wish I had a dog like his."

Twisting in her chair, Holly reached out to him. "Honey, you're supposed to be resting."

"I know, but I heard you talking." The boy stumbled closer and leaned into his mom. "Are you mad at Mark?"

Avoiding the question, she pulled him onto her lap. For now, at least, her ten-year-old son occasionally tolerated a motherly show of affection, especially as the aftereffects of a seizure drained his reserves. "It isn't Mark I should be upset with," she said with mock severity. "You should never have been playing over there."

Davey picked at a frayed thread where his jeans were wearing through the knees. "I like Shadow. It was like he could tell I was going to have a seizure."

A chill raced up her spine. "Really? How?"

"I don't know. He just sort of…knew. And then he stayed right beside me the whole time till Mark had to take him home."

Holly had read about service animals for people with epilepsy and had considered applying to get a dog for Davey when he was old enough to qualify. But the cost was far beyond her reach as a single mom, and waiting lists for a low-cost or free animal might take years.

"Samuel told me Shadow was Kellie's service dog," Joella said. "He's the smartest dog I've ever seen. And so gentle. Sophie's crawling now, and last night when Mark and Shadow came up to the apartment, Shadow wouldn't let Sophie past the edge of her floor quilt."

Sophie was Samuel's baby from a previous relationship, but Joella loved her like her own.

Holly furrowed her brow. "Who's Kellie?"

"Mark's daughter," Lindsey explained. "She died of a heart condition a few years ago."

Her heart ached for the man. "That's awful." It also explained the sadness in Mark's eyes earlier. Seeing Shadow watching over Davey the way the dog had surely done with his daughter must have evoked all kinds of painful memories.

Davey's mouth stretched wide in a gaping yawn, and his head sank against Holly's shoulder. She nudged him to his feet. "Let's get you back in bed, sweet boy. You need a nice, long nap."

If it wasn't the weekend, she'd be on the phone with Davey's doctor asking whether it was time to review his meds. She'd call her Monday for sure.

She also hoped for an opportunity to offer Mark Caldwell the apology she owed him—if he'd even speak to her after she'd practically thrown him out.

Tucking Davey back in bed, she pondered taking him straight home. Between losing their building contractor and worrying about her son, she felt on the verge of a breakdown—one she could ill afford with not only Davey but her two best friends from high school counting on her.

Get hold of yourself, Holly. Quietly closing the bedroom door, she whispered the words of her late grandmother's favorite psalm: *This is the day which the Lord hath made; we will rejoice and be glad in it.*

"We should enjoy *every* day," Gran used to say, "because we never know what tomorrow will bring."

You were so right, Gran. Being a widow and single mom struggling to make ends meet had certainly never been part of Holly's plan. She and Blaine were supposed to raise their family and grow old together in their cozy two-story Colonial in Waxahachie, until a fatal car accident on icy roads ended those dreams.

It was Blaine who had encouraged her to dream again. After too many aching disappointments, including losing her beloved grandmother to cancer, she'd decided it was better living in the present and accepting each day as it came.

Then Blaine had walked into her life. He'd approached the serving table at the wedding reception her employer was catering and asked her which entrée she recommended.

"You should definitely try the beef stroganoff," she'd answered with a smile.

"And why is that?"

Her reply might have sounded a teensy bit smug. "Because it's my recipe."

He'd taken one bite, and his eyes rolled back in his head. "Wow." He leaned closer, his warm gaze curling Holly's toes. "Will you marry me?"

Not six months later, she'd done exactly that.

Then, four years ago, a knock at her front door had ripped open her heart and turned her whole world upside down. If Davey hadn't survived the accident, she'd have had nothing left to live for.

Last spring, the opportunity to join Lindsey and Holly to run River Bend Events had seemed like a dream come true. Without Blaine, the house in Waxahachie was just that—a house. Moving to Gabriel Bend would give both her and Davey a new start.

And maybe…someday…she'd have the means to follow the one dream that had lingered since childhood—opening her own ladies' tearoom, like the one Gran used to take her to every year on her birthday.

Shoulders heaving, she brushed a stray tear from her

cheek. With Davey napping, she might as well help her friends find a new contractor.

When she passed the kitchen doorway, Audra had just come inside. "There's a little black dog scratching and whining to get in the house. I could barely squeeze past him. Any idea who he belongs to?"

"It must be Mark Caldwell's dog." Holly detoured through the kitchen and peered out the glass in the back door. What on earth was the little guy doing over here again?

Then she glimpsed Mark striding across the backyard. Dragging stiff fingers through his thick brown hair, he looked none too happy about having to chase down his wayward pet. She was about to duck out of sight when Mark stepped onto the porch and their gazes met through the glass. Too late to pretend she hadn't seen him. She should go out there right now and clear the air between them.

Great. She *would* be looking out the window just now. Mark sighed. All he wanted was to leash his dog and go. He had enough on his mind without another confrontation with a beautiful mom wearing a major chip on her shoulder.

Beautiful? He'd better nip those notions in the bud pronto.

He bent to seize Shadow's collar, but the dog skittered out of reach. "Boy, don't do this to me."

The door opened. When Holly stepped out, quickly pulling the door closed behind her, Shadow plopped down at her feet, an expectant expression in his ebony eyes.

She glanced at the dog, then arched a brow as she looked up at Mark. "I see you lost your dog again. It doesn't seem very *responsible* of you to let him go roaming by himself."

"Touché." Guess he deserved having his words thrown back in his face, even though she'd delivered them with more kindness than he had. "What I said earlier—I had no right."

"But you weren't wrong. I should have been paying more attention to where Davey was playing." She inhaled softly, arms crossed over her abdomen. "I truly am grateful you and your dog were there."

"Me, too." He really needed to stop letting those soulful green eyes of hers affect him like they did. "Is Davey doing better?"

"He's napping. He's usually very tired after a seizure."

"How often does this happen…if you don't mind me asking?"

"His last one was a few months ago. He may need his meds adjusted. I'll be calling his doctor first thing Monday."

"That's a good idea." Mark shuffled his feet. "I should, ah…"

Holly knelt to pet Shadow, who hadn't budged. "Hey, fella, did you come all the way over here to check on Davey? When he wakes up, I'll tell him you came by." One hand on Shadow's collar, she reached toward Mark and whispered, "Hand me the leash."

Seconds later, she'd secured Shadow and returned the leash to him.

"Thanks." If only Shadow would come peacefully now and Mark wouldn't have to drag him off the porch. "Sorry we bothered you. In Shadow's case, dogged determination—no pun intended—seems to go right along with massive intelligence."

"He's obviously a very special animal." Despite her brief smile, regret dimmed Holly's expression. "I'd give anything if Davey could have a service dog."

"Have you looked into getting one?" What was he doing, asking personal questions like this? And why did he care? Once he headed back to Montana in a couple of days—which at this point he fully intended—he'd probably never see Holly Elliot or her son again.

What were you thinking, Tito? You barely knew me, so how could you imagine I'd want any part of your horse ranch?

Holly had turned away slightly. Her shoulders heaved in another quiet sigh that whipped his attention back to the present. "Being a single mom, trying to make a decent living for us, I can't take on the expense of an ordinary pet, let alone apply for a service dog. And with Davey just wanting to be a normal kid—it's hard."

Mark swallowed. Kellie had just wanted to be a normal kid, too. "Is his dad in the picture? Maybe he could—"

"My husband's dead."

You walked right into that one, Caldwell. "Sorry, I didn't know."

"No reason you should." She hiked her chin. "Davey and I have been on our own for the last four years. I'm doing the best I can, but..." Her lower lip trembled.

Wonderful. She was about to cry, and Mark couldn't handle a woman's tears just now. Giving Shadow's leash a tug, he backed toward the porch steps. "Davey's a good kid. I'm sure you're doing fine. So, ah, I'll be going—"

"Wait." Sniffling, she used her knuckles to blot away the wetness gathering at the bridge of her nose. "I... I'd like to apologize for misjudging you. I didn't think you could possibly understand my situation, until..." She cast him a sad smile, continuing softly, "Lindsey told me you lost your daughter. I'm so very sorry."

"Yeah, thanks." Now he *really* needed to get out of here. He gave the leash another quick pull. "Let's go, boy."

She drew a quick breath. "Unless you're in a hurry, I—I mean *we*—were just talking about you and—"

Sure they were. After how he'd lit into Holly earlier, he wouldn't even guess what they'd been saying.

"And we wondered if you'd give us some advice about our building project."

Not what he expected. At all. The way she was looking at him with those kryptonite eyes, half hopeful, half scared, made it hard to think straight. "Wh-what did you want to know?"

"Maybe you could come inside for a few minutes?" She motioned behind her toward the door.

Don't do it, Caldwell. This is asking for way more involvement than you need.

"Okay, sure." He followed her through the kitchen. She took a left in the hallway, but Shadow tugged the leash to the right, toward the room where Davey must still be resting. "Not now, boy." To Holly, he said, "I take it this is about losing your building contractor?"

"Oh, you heard. He left us in a terrible bind." Holly showed Mark back into the study. Lindsey and Joella, seated at a worktable, both looked up with surprised smiles.

"Since Mark is here," Holly said, "I thought we could ask him our questions."

"Great!" Lindsey motioned toward one of the chairs. "Thanks, Mark."

He offered a polite nod. "Not sure how I can help, but ask away."

Though his cousins' wives did most of the talking, he found his gaze continually drifting toward Holly, who'd taken a chair across from him. He still felt like a heel for coming on so strong with her.

"We just don't want to start over from square one," Lindsey was saying.

"No, of course not." Mark drew a hand across his mouth and hoped his inattentiveness wasn't too obvious. "You'd want to hire someone you can bring up to speed pretty quickly. Someone who isn't bogged down with other commitments." He knew he'd kick himself later, but he asked anyway. "Maybe I could take a look at your specs?"

"Would you?" Lindsey sat forward. "That would be awesome!"

Joella stood. "I need to get home, but Lindsey and Holly can show you the plans."

Lindsey glanced at her watch. "Wow, it's later than I thought. I'm supposed to be helping Audra and Spencer with the livestock. Holly, would you mind?"

"*Me?* Um…okay." Her eyes widened in a deer-in-the-headlights look.

Mark knew a setup when he saw one. "I'll be around for a couple more days. We can try this again when everyone's available."

"No, please," Lindsey said as she followed Joella out. "We need to decide something pretty quick. Holly can fill you in. See y'all later!"

The sudden silence echoed. Swallowing, Mark turned to Holly. "So. The specs?"

This trip to Texas was definitely not going according to plan.

Chapter Two

If only Holly wouldn't keep looking at him that way—half hopeful, half annoyed—maybe he could actually think.

The building plans lay on the worktable, a pencil cup, paperweight and stapler holding down three of the corners. Holly secured the fourth corner while Mark perused the top sheet, which showed the foundation and plot survey. Focusing his attention, he then paged through to examine the floor and roof plans, electrical and plumbing schematics, renderings of the exterior, and construction notes.

A few minutes later, Shadow scrambled to his feet, the leash tightening on Mark's wrist. He glanced up to see Davey enter the room.

"You're back." Davey smiled and stifled a yawn. When Mark dropped the leash, Shadow darted over to the boy. Davey knelt, laughing as Shadow showered his face with doggy kisses. "Hey, fella. Miss me already?"

"Pretty sure he did," Mark said. "He hightailed it over here first chance he got."

Holly frowned at her son. "I thought you were sleeping."

"I slept some. I'm not tired anymore. Can I go out-side and play with Shadow?"

The kid's hopeful grin tugged at the hollow place in Mark's heart. He raised a brow in Holly's direction. "It's okay with me."

"I don't know…"

"How about if we *all* go? Those two can play, and you can show me the building site. I'd like to see what your contractor's already completed."

She nodded, looking almost relieved, as if she couldn't wait to escape being trapped in this room with him. Could he blame her?

They exited through the kitchen. Shadow, released from the leash, pranced around Davey like they were best buds. The dog snatched a stick he'd found near the porch steps and tried to get the kid to throw it.

As they crossed the backyard, Davey tossed the stick ahead of them for Shadow to retrieve. "Mom, can we get a dog like Shadow someday?"

"Honey, you know a pet isn't in the budget right now."

The boy's shoulders drooped. "That's what you al-ways say."

When he'd trotted farther ahead, Holly sighed. "He's right, and I feel awful that I can't give him what he wants—what he *needs*, really, because a service dog would be such a blessing, a companion for him and peace of mind for me. But I have a hard enough time making ends meet, and—" She cut herself off with a sniff. "Sorry, didn't mean to belabor my personal prob-lems."

"Sometimes it helps to vent." *Like you'd know.* He was the world's worst at opening up about his own troubles.

"It's not that my life is so awful. I love working with Lindsey and Joella, and Gabriel Bend is a charming place to live." Her mouth opened as if she had more to say, but then she clamped her lips together and went silent.

Fine with Mark. Didn't he have enough to sort out without allowing a pretty widow's issues to prey on his heart? He focused on watching Davey and Shadow take turns in some kind of fetch-the-stick relay. Shadow always enjoyed a good romp, but it had been a long time since Mark had seen him quite this frisky.

Face it. He misses Kellie as much as you do.

Joella and Lindsey both rushing off with more important things to do? *Yeah, right.* Holly's happily married best friends had made no secret of wanting the same for her. Didn't they get that she'd loved and lost the best guy ever? No one could replace Blaine in her heart.

And besides still grieving the loss of his daughter, Mark Caldwell appeared to have plenty of issues of his own. He wasn't exactly Mr. Personality, either. Not to mention he was likely to leave for Montana once he'd dealt with his grandfather's bequest.

As they reached the building site, she called to her son, "Stay where I can see you, okay?"

"Yes, ma'am." With a dramatic roll of his eyes, Davey picked up the stick Shadow had dropped at his feet.

Mark walked the perimeter of the concrete foundation. He stopped on the far side and set his fists on his hips. "How long has this been curing?"

Holly blinked as she mentally counted days. "A little over a week, I think."

He stepped onto the foundation and inspected the areas where plumbing and electrical lines had been roughed in. His stony expression gave no hint as to his opinion of the work completed thus far.

Moments later, he joined Holly on the driveway. "Can we go look at the plans again?"

"Sure." She led the way around to the back porch and instructed Davey not to leave the yard.

Mark shook his finger at the dog. "That goes for you, too, Shadow."

"Humph. We've all seen how well your dog obeys you," Holly said, reaching for the doorknob.

"About as well as your son listens to you."

The muttered comment made her neck muscles tighten. She turned to glare at the man behind her. "Look, if you're going to—"

"Sorry. I was *kidding*." Mark lifted both hands. "But then, I've never been known for my scintillating sense of humor."

Guilt brought heat to Holly's face. "I was actually kind of joking, too. Shadow's a pretty cool dog."

"Yeah, he is. And so's your son. A cool kid, I mean."

Holly suppressed a snicker at his near slip of the tongue. She motioned him through to the study.

Once again, he seemed lost in thought as he examined the plans. Holly kept waiting for him to say something, but all she got was an occasional grunt or *mmm-hmm*.

After reaching the last page, he rolled the plans and tapped them against his palm. "Mind if I borrow these? I'd like to look a little closer at a few things."

She looked at him askance. "Surely you don't want to spend your last few days with your family reviewing our building specs?"

"Really, it's not a problem." Exhaling slowly, he closed his eyes and used his index finger to massage the wrinkle between his narrowed brows. "Anyway, until I figure out some stuff, my travel itinerary is kind of fluid."

"Then, of course, feel free to take the plans." She gave an eye roll not unlike her son's earlier. "It doesn't appear we'll be needing them anytime soon."

"Great. I'll get them back to you in a day or so." He started down the hall.

She hurried to catch up. "So…are you even considering staying in town? I mean, I heard about the will—" She slapped her palm to her forehead. "Which is absolutely none of my business."

Jaw tightening, he stopped at the back door. "It's complicated."

"I'm sure it is." She backed up a step and wished she'd never raised the question. "I'll be praying for your decision. And thanks in advance for any contractor advice you can give us."

"Sure." Mark paused and turned. "We should probably trade phone numbers, in case I need more information from you. Unless you'd rather I deal directly with Lindsey or Joella?"

"No, they've apparently delegated the assignment to me." With a resigned sigh, she tugged her cell phone from her sweater pocket. Why did the thought of giving her contact info to this grumpy but easy-on-the-eyes near stranger make her all shivery inside? She had no reason not to trust him—the entire Navarro clan would surely vouch for his character. She hoped he didn't notice the slight tremor in her hands as they exchanged phones to key in their numbers.

Reclaiming his cell, Mark pocketed it. Without looking her way, he walked out to the porch and called to his dog.

Davey came around from the side of the house, Shadow at his heels. "Aw, does he have to go home already?"

"Afraid so." Leash in hand, Mark marched down the steps. "You don't want to see what happens when this boy's supper is late."

Holly smirked. Hard not to notice his tone with Davey was so much friendlier than the one he used with her.

As Mark and his dog crossed the field toward the barbed-wire fence, Davey trudged to the porch and plopped down on the top step. "Why won't you let me have a dog, Mom? Dad would have said yes. You're just being mean."

His accusation stabbed her heart. A knot in her throat, she pointed across the yard. "Get in the van. We're going home."

"To our dumb old apartment? There's *nothing* fun to do there. Why can't we—"

"Davey! Enough. I'm going inside to get my purse, and you'd better be buckled in your seat—and with a *much* improved attitude—by the time I come out."

Lord, help. Things were supposed to get better after their move to Gabriel Bend, and mostly they had. But Davey's disobedience lately—was it simply part of growing up and asserting his independence? Or had Holly been trying too hard to keep her son close, to protect the one constant in her life when so much had been ripped away?

Davey's longing for his own dog wasn't a new thing. Shortly after his birth, when Holly and Blaine had moved from their tiny starter home in Waxahachie into the three-bedroom Colonial with a spacious fenced yard, they'd often talked about getting a dog someday. Having more kids, too.

Unconsciously, her hand went to her abdomen. *I'm sorry, Blaine. I'm so, so sorry.*

Good thing Shadow hadn't resisted being leashed this time, or Mark didn't know how he'd get the dog to return with him.

Worse, his sort-of apology for criticizing Holly's parenting skills hadn't exactly been artful. Then, caught up in the building plans, he'd been his usual brusque self. Face it, tactful communication under pressure definitely wasn't his strong suit—hence his broken marriage. And hadn't Kellie chastised him often enough about his bluntness when the doctors and nurses didn't seem to be doing all they could to treat her? Her innate kindness, despite how sick she was, shamed him.

Forget Tito's ultimatum—Mark had no business contemplating staying on at Navarro Quarter Horses, much less involving himself in these unfinished building projects. He should head straight back to Montana and the construction crew he'd left his foreman to oversee. Not that he had any qualms about Bob's competence—the guy had been his right-hand man for a good ten years now—but Mark didn't handle downtime well. On most projects, he preferred to work alongside his crew, hefting a hammer, smelling the sawdust, grouting tile. Before he'd left for Texas, they'd been making good progress on a new two-story office building for a local insurance firm. By now, the crew would have begun putting up drywall.

Maybe he'd take off first thing tomorrow and use the long drive home to clear his head. Except he really needed to stick around long enough to sign whatever papers were required to refuse his inheritance. Besides, his parents' flight wasn't until Monday evening, and Mom might need extra moral support for deciding what to do with the ugly old cabin. Considering Tito's failing mental faculties over the past year, Mom most likely had grounds to contest the terms. But would she? Probably not.

The next morning, Mark made his excuses about skipping church. His parents knew full well how he felt about God and religion since Kellie died. After a walk with Shadow, he settled in for another round with the plans for the event center. He'd asked to see Samuel and Joella's house specs, too. *Just doing a favor for my cousins*, he kept telling himself.

Before he knew it, the afternoon was half-gone. Stiff from hovering for hours over the plans spread across Aunt Lois's kitchen table, he took Shadow outside for a little playtime. He found his dad in one of the Adirondack chairs surrounding the backyard firepit.

His father closed the cover of his e-reader. "Wondered if you'd be surfacing anytime soon."

"Been a little preoccupied." Mark tossed a tennis ball for Shadow, then slumped into the chair next to his father's.

Retrieving the ball, the dog bypassed Mark and dropped it in his dad's lap. Dad laughed and flung the ball across the yard. "I think he gave up on you."

"Guess I have been pretty boring lately."

His father tilted his head and cast Mark a meaningful frown. "I hope it means you've been giving serious thought to your next move."

"You mean about the will? No way I can stay here, Dad. My job—"

"Which is *just* a job. You know you've only been filling time since Kellie died."

"Dad, don't."

"No, son. Listen to me. Maybe this is a chance for you to take stock of your life and regain some perspective."

Mark released a derisive laugh. "But here, of all places? I'm a builder, not a rancher."

"Have you forgotten you'd have not one but two building projects already in the works? You'd be helping your family…and yourself."

The back door opened, and his mother came out with a coffee mug. The aroma of Aunt Lois's cinnamon-laced coffee teased his senses. "Here, thought you might need this."

He did. Badly. "Thanks, Mom."

Offering a wry half smile, she tucked a loose strand of dark hair into her silver-streaked French twist. "I know that look. What are you two at odds about this time—or do I even need to ask?"

"Dad's trying to convince me to stay."

"Maybe you should."

Her bluntness made Mark stiffen. "Why should I care a whit about this ranch, much less being a Navarro, especially after Tito left you nothing but a run-down old cabin?"

"Because—" Chin lifted, Mom reached for Dad's hand before continuing softly, "Because there remains more to be done here to put the past to rest, and my heart is telling me that task will fall to you."

"Me? I don't understand." He glanced between his parents, but they merely smiled sadly as if guarding a solemn secret.

While he gaped at them, Dad rose and tucked Mom

beneath his arm. "You'll figure it out, son." As they started toward the house, he added over his shoulder, "With God's help, you'll find your way."

Could they be any more cryptic? And really, like God would suddenly start caring about Mark's problems.

Still…his father had a point. Since losing Kellie, he hadn't bothered with much of a life beyond work. Bob had been talking for a while about wanting more of a stake in their construction business. Maybe the man would consider buying him out completely.

But submit to his grandfather's conditions and stay on at Navarro Quarter Horses for a year? Not a choice he could ever have pictured himself making.

The next morning, after helping his parents load their luggage into the trunk of the rental car, Mark stooped to give his petite mother a hug. "Wish you weren't leaving for the airport already."

"I want to do some shopping in Austin before our flight."

It was an excuse. Mom had never spent any more time at the ranch than necessary. "Buy me a present?"

She laughed and reached up to pat his cheek. "You're too old for presents. Anyway, we won't be seeing you for a while."

"Yeah, I forgot." His jaw clenched. Sometime between Saturday and this morning, he'd convinced himself he needed to stick around and see where things went.

"This is the right decision, *mijo*. I'm glad you're taking more time to consider your next steps."

"And that's *all* I'm doing—thinking about it." With a wry grin, he turned to accept a manly embrace from his dad. "Don't be surprised if I'm back in Missoula this time next month."

"Wouldn't hurt to pray about it," his father advised. "We'd miss you, but you might actually like living in Texas. A lot less snow to shovel, for one thing. Did you see the forecast we're flying home to?"

"You know you love it. Quit complaining." Choosing to ignore the prayer comment, Mark gave his dad a good-natured punch to the arm, then moved aside so Uncle Hank and Aunt Lois could offer their goodbyes. As his father turned the car around and headed toward the road, Mark lifted one hand in a wave.

With Aunt Lois returning to the house and Uncle Hank traipsing off to do whatever a quarter horse rancher usually did this time of day, Mark remained in the driveway, his thoughts racing. After thoroughly examining both the River Bend Events building plans and those for Samuel and Joella's new home, he had to admit he was intrigued. Nothing lit a fire in his blood like envisioning how one-dimensional construction drawings could be transformed into functionally appealing structures of brick, wood and steel.

Which he could do equally well in Missoula. There wasn't anything uniquely special about the event center or Samuel's house that should give him reason to sell his business and uproot himself. Not even the chance to inherit a third of a half of a quarter horse ranch. What did that come to, anyway—one-sixth? Good thing "quarter horse" didn't literally mean one-fourth of a horse!

Groaning, he checked the time on his phone. Was it too early to give the family attorney a call?

A nudge to his kneecap drew his attention to Shadow. Tongue hanging out, the dog plopped down in front of him, his gaze shifting between Mark's face and the house next door.

"No," he scolded, hands on hips. "We're not going over there. It's Monday. Davey will be in school."

Shadow whined and pawed Mark's sneaker.

"What am I gonna do with you, fella?" Squatting, he ruffled the dog's feathery cheek fur.

Footsteps on gravel sounded behind him. He rose to find Samuel coming his way, little Sophie bundled against his chest. "Sorry I missed saying goodbye to your folks," his cousin said. "Mornings with a baby can get pretty hectic."

"No kidding." Though it had been almost fifteen years, how well Mark remembered. He tugged on the string of Sophie's pink fleece hoodie, eliciting a giggle.

Over Samuel's shoulder, Mark glimpsed Joella coming out of the barn, a large leather tote on her arm. She smiled and strode over. "I'll be working next door with Holly and Lindsey most of the day. Whenever you have time, we'd love to talk more with you about our event center project."

He nodded. "I'll be over later this morning."

A brief conversation with the family attorney assured him he didn't have to make any hasty decisions about his inheritance. Considering his state of mind, it was probably just as well.

By ten thirty he was pulling up a chair to join the three women at their worktable in the study. Naturally, Shadow wouldn't be left behind. Stretched out on the floor between Mark's chair and Holly's, the dog kept staring up at her as if hoping she'd somehow produce Davey so they could play some more.

Mark was having a hard time keeping his eyes to himself. Holly looked especially pretty this morning, her face dewy and makeup-free and her ash-brown waves pulled into a high ponytail. A couple of loose tendrils framed her temples in a casually messy sort of way that tightened his belly.

He cleared his throat and turned his attention to the building specs. "So…these look good."

Lindsey and Joella exchanged glances with Holly, then peered at him across the table. "That's it?" Joella asked.

"I mean, everything's in order. Whoever you hire to take over should be able to step right into the project."

The women went silent.

Avoiding their penetrating stares, he leaned back and stretched out his legs. "Listen, it's not as simple as you think. I'm licensed in Montana. To work as a general contractor here, I'd need to check local requirements— business registration, permits, insurance, whatever. That'd take time."

Still, they didn't speak. Their enigmatic smiles said plenty.

"Okay, okay. Give me a couple of days to look into it. But no promises."

Audible sighs of relief surrounded him. "Thank you!" Joella said. "That's all we can ask."

He figured they'd like to ask plenty more of him, but they were polite enough to back off. "Mind if I keep these plans a little longer? I might need to refer to them."

"They're all yours," Lindsey stated, clearly implying more than merely a yes to his request.

He rolled up the plans and stood to go.

Holly pushed her chair back. "I need to be going, too. Davey has a doctor's appointment in Round Rock right after lunch."

"Let us know how it goes. Oh, and Holly?" Joella

tapped the table. "Be sure to tell Mark your idea about enlarging the kitchen space."

Glancing at Holly, he skewed his lips. "Any adjustments need to be factored in sooner rather than later."

"I know." Looping her arm through her shoulder bag, she heaved a helpless shrug. "We'd planned to discuss a few changes with Jay Graham last week, before we found out he couldn't complete the job."

"We can talk about it next time I see you." He followed her out through the kitchen. "Will you be back this afternoon?"

"Probably not. Davey's doctor is all the way over in Round Rock, and Austin-area traffic anywhere near I-35 is always terrible."

"Oh, right. I hope the appointment goes well. Maybe tomorrow, then? You have my number."

And what made him suddenly want to bend over backward to make things right for a woman he hardly knew?

Dr. Liggett, a fiftysomething woman with short, silver-blond hair, gave Davey a general exam and reviewed his meds. She glanced over at Holly. "You said this was a relatively mild seizure?"

Davey gave his head an annoyed shake. "It was hardly nothing."

"Hardly *anything*," Holly corrected. "It happened when he was out playing by himself, so I didn't see it. A…a neighbor found him and brought him to me." Why did she feel so embarrassed admitting that?

The doctor perused Davey's records on her computer screen. "His meds are right at the levels they should be for a boy his age and size, so I'd rather not tinker with dosages at this point. But there could be other factors at play." With a friendly smile at Davey, she said she'd like to discuss some "grown-up stuff" with his mother and had the nurse take him out to a waiting area.

Once they were alone, Dr. Liggett rolled her stool directly in front of Holly, her expression filled with warm concern. "Breakthrough seizures can be triggered by all kinds of things, including stress. Is there anything that could be causing extra anxiety for either one of you?"

Tears pricked the backs of Holly's eyes. Things had been stressful for a while now—ever since her husband died, to be honest. She bolted the door on those memories and sat a little straighter. "Some days I feel so much pressure as a single mom. And lately Davey's been acting out more, doing things I specifically told him not to, for his own safety. Maybe if I wasn't so busy with the event venue and could spend more time with him—"

"I didn't mean for you to go blaming yourself." Dr. Liggett patted Holly's knee. "But perhaps it's time you got some help."

"*Help?* You mean like counseling?"

"That's always an option. But actually, I was thinking along the lines of a male role model for Davey. Does he have an uncle or a close family friend who could fill those shoes?"

"My business partners' husbands have been very good with Davey. I suppose I could ask if they'd spend more time with him." Except they had plenty going on in their own lives—Samuel was office manager for Navarro Quarter Horses, and Spencer still worked there part-time while also operating New Start Equine Rescue and assisting Lindsey and Audra with their cattle.

Holly left the office with a promise to think more about the doctor's suggestion. She could certainly appreciate the need for a positive male influence in Davey's life. There were days when it was clear how much he missed his dad.

I miss you, too, Blaine. If only I could take that day back...

As she and Davey walked out to the minivan, her cell phone chimed with an incoming text from Joella: If you have time after Davey's appointment, we need to iron out a few more details for the Gracey-Totten wedding.

As taxing as this day had been, she'd looked forward to chilling out at home, but she couldn't blow off client business. The sixtysomething couple's second-time around romance had tugged at Holly's heartstrings from the very first meeting. After Harvey Gracey had lost his first wife to cancer, he'd joined a grief support group at his church. There, he'd met Nancy Totten, whose husband had also recently passed away. Neither had expected to fall in love again—much less remarry—but their hearts had other ideas. On the Friday before Christmas, just a few weeks away, they would pledge their lives to each other in the chapel before a small gathering of family and closest friends.

Perhaps if Holly and Blaine had had more time together, another twenty or thirty or forty years to see their children grow up, marry, have children of their own...

But no, not even a lifetime of making memories together could have lessened the pain of losing her husband. She couldn't imagine ever loving anyone the way she'd loved Blaine. Better to cherish the years they'd had and be the best mom she could to their son.

She thumb-typed a quick reply: On my way.

Chapter Three

~

At the ranch, she'd barely pulled into the parking area behind the chapel when Davey asked, "Can I go see if Shadow can play till you're done?"

"Oh, Davey, I'm not sure you should bother Mr. Caldwell."

He crossed his arms and glared. "I wouldn't have to bother him if you got me my own dog."

She glared right back. "Haven't I told you about adjusting your attitude?"

"Okay, okay." He screwed his mouth into a pout. "But can I go over there and ask? Please?"

Casting a glance skyward, she gave her head a quick shake, then took her cell phone from her purse. "Let me call first and make sure he doesn't mind."

Davey pumped his fist and released a muted *"Yes!"*

As she searched for the number Mark had entered in her contacts, Dr. Liggett's suggestion played through her thoughts. Her son could benefit so much from building a relationship with an attentive and responsible adult male.

What about Mark? He clearly got along with Davey, and he knew something about taking care of a child with health concerns. Add his not only fun-loving but perceptive dog into the mix, and it could be a winning combination.

If he stayed in Gabriel Bend long enough to make it work.

And if he didn't? Her finger hovered over the call button.

"Mom."

Startled by her son's interruption, she hit the button by accident. Next thing she knew, Mark answered.

"Um, hi. It's—it's Holly." Her tongue got all twisted behind her teeth. "I had to come back to the ranch after all, and Davey was wondering if he could visit Shadow…"

"Sure. He would love the company. I've been tied up with other things most of day and haven't given him much attention."

Davey must have overheard. His excited bouncing shook the whole van.

She motioned for him to settle down. "Oh, good. I mean, *not* good you've had to ignore him. But good that—"

"I get it." Mark snorted. "I need to stretch my legs, so what if I walk over with Shadow in a few minutes? If you have time, you can tell me about those changes you wanted to make to the building plans."

"Oh, right. Thank you." Disconnecting, she left Davey waiting on the back porch while she went inside to tell Joella and Lindsey she'd join them shortly.

By the time she returned to the porch, Mark was crossing the field, Shadow bounding ahead of him. Davey jumped up to greet his new furry friend, and they were chasing each other around the backyard before Mark caught up.

One hand on his hip, the other clutching the building plans, he stood on the step below Holly as he watched the boy and dog. "I think I've been replaced."

"Not necessarily. Shadow probably just needs the occasional romp with someone…"

Mark turned toward her, one eye narrowed. "Don't you dare say *younger*."

She smirked. "Okay, I won't say it out loud."

"Ha-ha." Then his expression turned serious. "So what did the doctor say about Davey's seizure? Will his meds need to be changed?"

"No, but…" Ignoring the tremor in her belly, Holly rushed on before she could talk herself out of her request. "There's something I'd like to ask you—that is, if you do decide to stay in Gabriel Bend for a while…"

"What is it?"

She took another bolstering breath, then blurted, "Davey's doctor said it could help so much if he had a male mentor in his life. And you and Davey seem to hit it off, and obviously he's having a blast with Shadow. So I was wondering…" Running out of words, she cast him a pleading look hoping he'd get the message.

She hadn't noticed the color of his eyes until now, but as he gazed at her, they seemed to change from a dusky grayish brown to something more like the ocean in winter. His throat worked and he parted his lips as if to reply before clamping them shut again. He shook his head and glanced away.

"I'm so sorry," she said, wringing her hands. "We hardly know each other, and that was terribly presumptuous of me. Please, forget I asked."

"No…no, it's all right." His whole body seemed to sag, even as a tentative smile returned. "You flatter me, that's all."

Davey and Shadow ran up just then, both of them panting and out of breath. "Hey, Mark," he said, "does Shadow know any tricks?"

"Several, actually." Mark's eyes shuttered briefly. "Let me finish talking to your mom and I'll get him to show you a few. He performs his best for treats, though, and I didn't bring any with me."

"Mom, do you think Aunt Audra has anything we could give him?"

She shrugged. "I saw some cheese sticks in her fridge this morning."

"Shadow loves cheese," Mark said. "Just not too much at a time."

"Yay! Be right back." Davey gave Shadow a pat and then raced inside.

Holly made a mental note to replace what her son used. Alone on the porch with Mark, she pulled her lower lip between her teeth. "So…would you maybe think about mentoring Davey? For his sake?" *And mine?*

Shadow gave a yip, as if trying to convince Mark, too. One paw lifted, the dog whined and panted and stared up at him.

Exhaling sharply, he knelt to pet his dog. "Guess we all know what your answer would be, huh, fella? And somehow you always seem to get your way." Rising again, he faced Holly. "If things work out, sure, I could set aside regular times to spend with your son."

"Really?" Relief bubbled up in Holly's chest. "Thank you."

He replied with a quick smile, then lifted the plans. "You want to talk about these now, or later?"

Davey burst out the back door with a fistful of cheese sticks. When Holly frowned, he said, "It's okay, Mom. I asked Aunt Lindsey before I took them."

"That was smart." She turned to Mark. "Would you mind showing Davey some of Shadow's tricks while I deal with client business? It shouldn't take too long."

"Fine with me."

It turned out Nancy Totten had added a few names to the guest list, which meant extra seating and food. Once they'd covered the details, Holly donned her sweater and returned outside.

Mark was demonstrating to Davey how Shadow could balance a piece of cheese on his nose, then fling it into the air and catch it in his mouth. The boy laughed and applauded. "Wow, can I try?"

"Sure." Mark pinched off a bite of cheese. Glancing Holly's way, he told Davey, "Why don't you practice for a few minutes while I go over some stuff with your mom?"

"Talented dog," she said with an appreciative smile.

"He likes to show off." Mark nodded across the driveway. "Mind if we walk over to the building site? I tend to think better in three dimensions."

Moments later, they stood on the foundation where the new kitchen would be. Holly studied the floor plan spread open between Mark's hands—strong, capable hands, callused and scarred from honest hard work.

She gave herself a stern mental shake and pointed to the kitchen area on the drawing. "I was thinking if we made the storage room a little smaller, it would give us room for a larger fridge, plus another foot or two of counter space."

Mark nodded. "Looks doable. No load-bearing walls involved, and it shouldn't interfere with the plumbing and electrical lines."

"Would it add much to the cost?"

"Regarding construction, negligible. But appliance costs would be outside the scope of my part in this."

Her brows shot up. "That sounds awfully like you're agreeing to take on the project."

Edging a few steps away, he furled the plans. A tormented look clouded his expression. "Like I said before, there's a lot to take into consideration."

"The decision to leave behind everything familiar isn't easy, I know." Arms folded across her sweater, Holly turned toward the backyard, where Davey was carefully balancing a cheese bite on Shadow's nose. After everything they'd been through, it warmed her heart to see her son so happy.

"My parents seem to think staying would be good for me," Mark said with a humorless laugh. "They may know me better than I know myself."

She shifted to face him. "Then maybe you should listen to them."

A long sigh raked through him. "Yeah, maybe I should. Which means I need to get cracking on the details."

"If there's anything I can do…"

"Actually, there is…" He looked down at her. "I did some preliminary research today on state and county contractor regs. But it would be helpful if you could put me in touch with Jay Graham. Tell him I'd like contact info for his crew and subcontractors."

A hopeful flutter lifted her heart. "I'll call him before I leave today."

When they reached the back porch steps, Mark called Shadow. "Enough for now, guys. Davey, come see us next time you're at the ranch."

"Cool!" Her son's face lit up. "Are you gonna show me more of Shadow's tricks?"

"Absolutely."

Catching Mark's eye, Holly mouthed a sincere *thank-you*.

"My pleasure." As Davey ran off to play, he lowered his voice. "Glad there weren't any lingering effects after Saturday."

"Nope, he's back to his normal self—in more ways than one," she added with a disgruntled frown. "His attitude lately is enough to turn my hair gray."

"He's just being a ten-year-old kid. Cut him some slack."

Holly arched a brow. "Weren't you all over my case the other day about how I should be keeping closer tabs on him?"

"Don't remind me." Wincing, Mark flashed her an embarrassed grin. "How about this... When it comes to how you raise your kid, I promise to keep my mouth shut from now on."

"Don't worry about it. Besides," she added with a rueful laugh, "you and Shadow seem to be Davey's new best friends."

His expression softened. "I like him, too. As for Shadow, that goes without saying." He tucked the plans beneath his arm. "Well. I have more calls to make."

"Me, too. I'll get those names and numbers to you ASAP."

Watching him go, she decided there was much more to the man than what his gruff demeanor might suggest. Spencer had said Mark had a good heart, which he'd already demonstrated with his kindness toward Davey, not to mention his obvious affection for Shadow. Just the other day, Holly had been browsing Ally & Aiden Gifts in town and had come across a decorative sign that read If My Dog Trusts You, Then So Do I.

There was some logic in the statement—so long as there weren't any dog-friendly cat burglars on the loose.

The back door opened, and Lindsey peeked out. "Did he leave already? How'd it go?"

"Fine. He said the changes are doable."

Joella swung the door wider, squeezing in beside Lindsey. "And?"

"Don't quote me on this, but I *think* we may have a new contractor."

She prayed she wasn't wrong, because every day the building site sat idle meant that much longer until River Bend Events could expand their offerings and increase revenue. And Holly desperately needed that extra income to cover the rising cost of health insurance and Davey's ongoing medical expenses.

There was reason to hope, though. Not only did it look like Mark would take over the building project, but now Davey had a mentor and friend.

And someday, God willing, maybe Holly could save enough for her tearoom. It would be a tribute to her dear grandmother, who had inspired her love of cooking and her dream of giving other women, young and old, the gift of feeling as special as she'd always felt at her birthday luncheons with Gran.

Davey needs to feel special, too, you know. And for more affirming reasons than having a seizure disorder. If Mark could do that for her son, she'd be doubly grateful.

Lunch with her two best friends—now three, counting Audra—was almost as special as Holly's childhood birthdays with her grandmother. The next day, she whipped up a light and fluffy spinach quiche using a recipe she'd recreated based on memories of the tearoom Gran used to take her to.

Scraping the last crumbs from her plate, Lindsey moaned with pleasure. "This was amazing!"

"Seriously, Holly," Joella chimed in, "you need to patent this. Or whatever chefs do with recipes."

"Thanks. Glad you enjoyed it." Beaming, she rose and began clearing the table.

"Let me," Audra said. "The chef shouldn't have to do the dishes."

Holly wouldn't complain. She needed to take off early anyway to run some errands before picking up Davey from school.

On her way out to the minivan, her cell phone rang. Please, not another robocall trying to sell her an extension on her car warranty. How many of those had she blocked in the last year?

But no, the display registered Mark's name and number. *Please don't let him say he's changed his mind and is going back to Montana.* Which would disappoint her more—losing him as a contractor, or as Davey's mentor?

Or…another reason entirely?

Slamming the door on that thought, she willed professional calm into her tone as she answered. "Hi, Mark. How's it going?"

"Moving right along. Thanks for those contact numbers. I've had some informative discussions with Mr. Graham." The rumble of his deep, masculine voice made her stomach somersault. "Um, do you have a minute?"

"I'm on my way into town. Did you need something else?"

He cleared his throat. "I thought if you'd be bringing Davey back to the ranch later, maybe he and I could hang out."

"Oh." Holly opened the minivan door and flung her briefcase across to the passenger seat. She hadn't planned to return with Davey today—she had laundry and housecleaning to catch up on, plus mail to sort and bills to pay.

But then, if she divulged all that, he'd probably say forget it, and an afternoon of bonding with Davey might tip the scales for keeping Mark in Gabriel Bend.

Or break her son's heart next week or next month when Mark decided to pack his bags and return to Montana with Shadow.

"Hello? You still there?"

"Yes. Sorry." She scooted in behind the steering wheel. "I was just mentally sorting out a couple of things to make this afternoon work."

"If you have other plans, I totally get it—"

"No. It's nothing that can't wait." So what if she wore the same jeans and sweatshirt again tomorrow? "And I know Davey would be thrilled. I could be back by three thirty or so. Shall I drop him off next door?"

"Shadow and I will be watching for you."

While Mark waited for Holly and Davey to arrive, he strolled with Shadow out to the barn office, hoping Samuel could give him some insight into what he'd be facing if he committed to a year on the ranch.

"It isn't only about the horses," Samuel said in reply. "Otherwise, I'd be in trouble."

Mark spied the glass coffeepot on the warmer, an inch or so of dark brew in the bottom. He poured the remains into a clean mug and took a careful sip. Strong and bitter, and definitely not Aunt Lois's special blend.

"But you grew up on the ranch. Even though you left after college, I figured horses had to be in your blood."

"My dad and brother are naturally gifted horsemen. Me? Not so much." Samuel chuckled. "Why do you think I'm sitting behind this desk?"

"Well, I'm not a horseman, and I'm definitely not a desk guy, so where does that leave me?" Mark stepped around Shadow and took a seat.

Scratching his beard, Samuel leaned back in his chair. "I don't recall anything in the wording of Tito's will that said you had to be directly involved with the horse business. Didn't it just say 'live and work at the ranch for one year'? That could cover a lot of territory."

A grin crept across Mark's face. "Including building a house for my cousin and his family?"

"Exactly. And what would stop you from operating your own construction company from here? Once my house is done, you could have the apartment upstairs— plenty big for a single guy and his dog."

Mark swirled the dregs in his mug. "Sounds good in theory. On the other hand, I'm pretty sure Tito intended for me to actually learn something about the ranch he'd poured his life into, not just technically fulfill the terms of his will."

"You have a point." His cousin cast him a probing stare. "I guess the real question is, do you want to try?"

Jaw clenched, Mark absently stroked Shadow's head. "I keep asking myself what I'd ever do with a share of a horse ranch."

"Maybe Tito hoped spending a year here would help you figure that out."

At the sound of tires on gravel, Mark looked toward the window. A teal-green older-model minivan had just driven up. Shadow was already whining and pawing at the door. "That must be Holly. I told her I'd spend some time with Davey this afternoon."

"That's a nice thing you're doing," Samuel said. "Holly's a great mom, but sometimes she gets overwhelmed."

He paused at the door. "How well do you know her?"

"Considering she's been best friends with Joella and Lindsey since high school, I've gotten to know her fairly well in the months since she moved here." A smile narrowed Samuel's eyes. "Anything in particular you're curious about?"

It probably wasn't fair to probe for details behind Holly's back. Still… "Before I put my foot in my mouth again, I was wondering how her husband died."

"Car accident." Samuel's expression turned grim. "Holly doesn't talk about it, but Joella told me. Davey was with him and suffered a head injury, which they think is what brought on his epilepsy."

"Wow, that's rough."

"It gets worse. Holly was pregnant at the time. The shock of losing her husband caused her to miscarry." Samuel looked toward the window. "She's waiting. You should get out there."

Mark suddenly didn't know if he could face her. Why had he asked a question that risked making him actually care, when the last few years had been all about *not* feeling?

Shadow's impatient yip snapped him out of his pity party.

"All right, all right. Hold your horses." He yanked open the door before he could talk himself out of it.

One hand on Davey's shoulder, Holly stood next to her minivan. Seeing Mark striding her way, she shaded her eyes against the afternoon sun and offered a hesitant smile. "I wasn't sure where to look for you."

"Sorry, I was in the barn office talking to Samuel."

Davey dropped to his haunches to greet Shadow. "Hey, fella, wanna play?"

"He has a tennis ball around here somewhere." Mark gestured toward the backyard.

As boy and dog ran off in search of the ball, Holly gave a soft laugh. "You should have seen Davey's face when I told him I was bringing him to see you and Shadow again. If he hadn't had his seat belt on, he'd have been ricocheting all over the van."

She was squinting, so he moved between her and the slanting sun. Now he could see her eyes better, which was possibly a huge mistake. "Is it okay if I offer him a snack? Aunt Lois made oatmeal cookies today."

"He'd love it. Just keep it under control, or he'll be on a sugar high all evening."

"Gotcha. Anything else I should know, like allergies or whatever?"

"Nope." Inching toward her vehicle, she cast a nervous glance toward the yard, where Davey and Shadow chased each other around the firepit. "So I'll be right next door. You have my number if you have any problems…or questions…or whatever."

Mark tucked his fingertips into his front pockets. "If you're not comfortable leaving him with me, I understand."

"It isn't you—and besides, this mentor thing was my idea." Hugging herself, Holly released a self-deprecating laugh. "I'm just being a nervous mom."

The twinge in Mark's belly said he was about to make a suggestion he'd likely regret. He said it anyway. "If it'd make you feel better, you could hang out with us today and decide whether this arrangement's going to be helpful."

"Well… I don't have any urgent event business I should be working on this afternoon." One eye on her son, she skewed her lips. "And the truth is, I haven't been spending as much quality time with Davey as I should."

"Then come with us. We can grab Lois's cookies and some bottled water, and then I thought we'd take a hike across the ranch." He'd been meaning to inspect the old cabin that now belonged to his mother and see if there was anything worth salvaging.

"A-Across the ranch?" Now she *really* looked uneasy. "I hoped there'd be something you and Davey could do right here, where it's…"

"Safe?" With a shake of his head, he turned to watch the boy and dog wrestling in the grass. "See those two bundles of unbridled energy? They don't care about *safe*. They just want to have fun. So would you rather risk Davey going exploring on his own again, or let me take him on a supervised adventure?"

"You're right." Her shoulders lifted in a deep inhalation. She exhaled slowly. "When you put it that way, it makes a lot of sense."

"Then if it's a go, I'll run inside and get those snacks."

She gave a brief nod, and after a quick trip to the kitchen, he returned with a knapsack looped over one shoulder. "Davey, Shadow, let's go for a walk."

The boy jumped up from the ground and jogged over, the dog prancing at his heels. "Wait—Mom, are you coming with us?"

"Yeah, I thought I would. Just this once, since y'all are still getting acquainted." Her smile looked slightly forced. "Is that okay?"

The boy gave a half-hearted shrug. "Whatever. Come on, Shadow! Race ya!" The pair took off down the lane.

"Davey—"

Mark ended Holly's frantic wave with a firm touch to her arm. "We'll be right behind him. Chill out, Mom." He reached into the knapsack. "Here, have a cookie."

Accepting the cookie, she cast him a sideways glance. "Trying to calm me with carbs?"

"If it works." He grinned and took a cookie for himself.

Why did those big green eyes of hers affect him like they did? Yep, inviting her along amounted to a huge lapse in good judgment, for which he'd likely pay dearly.

Agreeing to go along on this hike had probably been unwise. Dusting crumbs off her chin, Holly tried not to look at the tall, handsome man striding alongside her. The last time butterflies had invaded her stomach this bad was her first date with Blaine, and the fact that Mark could evoke such feelings made her cringe with guilt.

"Cookie not agreeing with you?"

Naturally, her emotions would be written all over her face. She finished the last bite and forced a swallow. "No, it's good. Just a bit…chewy." Actually, it was melt-in-your-mouth delicious, but she'd grabbed on to a quick and convenient explanation.

"Maybe this'll help." Mark loosened the cap on a bottle of water and passed it to her.

"Thank you." Taking a sip, she appreciated his consideration for how hard those bottle caps could be to open. Then, checking to see that Davey and Shadow were still in view, she asked, "Do we have a destination in mind?"

His slowness to respond drew her glance. The muscles in his jaw worked briefly. "My grandfather left my mother a small plot of land with an old cabin. I want to give it a closer look."

Old cabin? Her steps faltered. "Are you sure it's safe?"

"Don't worry. If it's in bad shape, I'll see that it's locked down tight or boarded up or whatever it'll take to secure it from a curious kid on the prowl."

He must have read her mind. Her son would need no encouragement to sneak away later and explore a hazardous location on his own.

Then her brain backtracked to what he'd said about the cabin being his mother's inheritance. Hank Navarro had gotten half the ranch and Alicia, his sister, received only an old cabin? What had Mark's mother done to earn such disfavor? Lindsey had confided that her father, Owen McClement, had once been in love with Alicia, but that had ended when Alicia finished high school and left the ranch to live with relatives in Colorado. An almost-forty-years-in-the-past romance between a Navarro and a McClement seemed weak justification for a father and daughter to remain so estranged.

Farther ahead, Davy scampered over to a fence. On the other side, two reddish-brown horses stretched their noses over to sniff his outstretched hand. Heart thumping, Holly was about to shout for him to be careful, but before she could, Shadow barked, and the horses backed off.

Mark touched her arm. "See…no need to panic. Shadow wouldn't let anything happen to him."

"Shadow can't protect him twenty-four/seven."

"Maybe not. But he can be right there at his side anytime Davey's here with me."

Relaxing slightly, Holly heaved a sigh. "Considering

how my son turns into a mini Daniel Boone every time I bring him out to the ranch, that's a comforting thought."

They caught up with Davey and Shadow, where Mark shared the cookies with Davey and gave Shadow a doggy treat before they continued down the lane. Ahead, another track branched off to the left, this one overgrown with weeds and looking as if it hadn't seen much use in recent years.

In the distance, she made out a weathered roofline. "Is that the cabin?"

"That's it." Lips tight, Mark exhaled sharply as he veered left and began picking his way along the barely visible tire ruts. "Watch your step."

Good thing she'd worn her sturdy sneakers today. "Should we be worried about snakes?"

"Too chilly. They'll be holed up somewhere warm."

Sticking close, Holly suppressed a shiver. "Like an old cabin?"

Mark gave a half snort, half chuckle. "Hey, Davey, see that cabin up ahead? You're not to go inside until I check it out. Got it?"

"Yes, sir." The boy dialed back his wild leaps through the weeds.

"Thank you," she murmured.

As they rounded a shallow bend in the lane, the front of the cabin came into view. It was definitely old but didn't appear as dangerously decrepit as Holly had feared.

Davey ran up to a grime-smeared window and tried to peer inside. "Wow, did pioneers live here?"

"I don't think it's been around that long," Mark answered. "Careful around the porch. We don't know what might be living under there."

As if on cue, something dark and furry scooted out

from beneath the far end and tore off through the brush. Shadow gave chase, but only until the creature vanished into a thick copse of live oaks and cedars.

Hand at her throat, Holly inched closer to Mark. "What was that?"

"It moved so fast I couldn't tell. Maybe a fox or skunk."

"A skunk—really? Aw, I missed it!" Davey jogged over to where Shadow sat staring toward the trees as if on guard duty.

"Just as well," Mark said. "I'd hate for your mom to have to give you a deskunking bath later."

A shudder raced up her spine. "The idea of a bathtub full of tomato juice? Ick!"

"Actually, tomato juice just masks the odor. You need a special veterinary product to completely get rid of it." He stepped gingerly onto the porch.

"Speaking from experience?" Holly jiggled one of the roof supports, relieved that the cedar post felt solid.

"Shadow had a skunk encounter on one of our hikes last summer. That's one reason he knew better than to pursue our little squatter." Testing each creaking board, Mark edged toward the door. He tried the rusty latch, and the door scraped inward.

He tugged his phone from his pocket and activated the flashlight feature. With a wary glance over his shoulder, he said, "Stay out here until I see what's inside." More forcefully, he added, "That means you, Davey."

Jacket zipped against the chilly November breeze, Holly stood on the packed ground in front of the porch and kept one eye on her son. Shadow had returned from his critter watch, ears pricked as Davey poked at clumps of weeds with a long stick. Hopefully, they wouldn't roust anything more alarming than a grasshopper.

Several minutes later, Mark emerged. "Not too bad," he said, brushing a cobweb from his sleeve. "Samuel told me the family had used it as a fishing cabin, although not in recent years. There's a branch of the river just beyond those trees."

Davey trotted over, his eyes wide. "Can I look inside now?"

"Not today. First I want to deep-six any creepy-crawly critters hiding out in there."

"But then afterward?" Holly's son bounced on his heels. "It'd be so fun to camp here. And maybe we could go fishing, too."

"We'll see." Mark scratched his earlobe. "Here's an idea. Maybe you could help me whip this place into shape—with your mom's permission, of course."

Davey spun around, hands clasped and his expression pleading. "Mom, can I? Please say yes!"

She furrowed her brow. A project the two of them could tackle together might be a good thing. "I'll think about it, but only *after* Mark assures me the cabin is critter-free."

"I'll get on that first thing tomorrow." He closed the door and stepped off the porch. Looking toward the western hills, he said, "Sun's going down. We'd better head back."

With Davey and Shadow running ahead, they started down the rutted lane.

After a few minutes, Holly tilted her head to offer Mark a smile. "I haven't seen my son so enthusiastic about anything in a long time. Thank you again for agreeing to this arrangement."

He looked at her askance. "So you've decided I can be trusted with your son?"

"I never really doubted it, but with Davey's epilepsy,

I can't help worrying. You know what it's like to have a child with special needs—" At his sharp intake of breath, she wished she could snatch back her words. "I'm so sorry," she whispered. "I didn't mean to—"

"Don't apologize." Facing forward, he adjusted the knapsack on his shoulder.

They reached the junction and turned right onto the wider lane. Davey and Shadow were already far ahead, but it was a fairly straight shot back to the house, so Holly relaxed her vigilance.

The silence between her and Mark grew awkward, at least on her part. With her thoughts jumping from one thing to another, she couldn't stop herself from broaching another topic. "What will you do with the cabin after you clean it up?"

"Not sure yet. Maybe I'll decide to make it livable enough to move in."

"Really? But it's out in the middle of nowhere. What about water? Plumbing and electricity?"

He cast her a droll grin. "I build houses for a living. I think I can figure it out."

She gave herself a mental facepalm. Time for a slight change of subject. "How are things looking for you to take over as our contractor?"

"Jay Graham brought me up to speed on both the event center and Samuel's house. Once I take care of the legalities of going into business here and line up the crews, we'll be able to get to work."

"That's wonderful. But…what about your construction business in Montana?"

Silence stretched again as Mark gazed across a pasture where several horses grazed. "I don't want to burn any bridges until I see how things go here."

So his decision to stay wasn't final. "You'll see our building projects through, though...won't you?"

"I'm not in the habit of backing out of commitments." His tight expression said she'd offended him.

How could he be so cordial one minute and so cross the next? "I never meant to suggest you were. But my partners and I have business objectives we hope to meet, and you can't blame us for wanting some assurance."

He stepped in front of her, then turned and halted. She skidded to a stop before plowing into him. Fists low on his hips, head down, he drew a long, slow breath before meeting her gaze. "I *assure* you, I will see both jobs to completion. You'll have it in writing by the end of the week."

Chapter Four

For the past four days, Mark had tried and failed to forget his totally unwarranted loss of cool Tuesday afternoon. He still wasn't sure what had set him off. Holly had had every right to push him for a clear commitment to the River Bend Events construction project.

He'd struggled to lower the temperature of his over-reaction before catching up with Davey—no reason to inflict his moodiness on the kid. Unfortunately, his goodbye to Holly had been only a few degrees above glacial. Not surprising she hadn't asked him again about spending time with her son. And probably just as well, because he was quickly getting attached to the kid, and if this Texas thing didn't work out, the ten-foot brick wall he'd built around his heart couldn't protect him from another goodbye.

In the meantime, he'd taken steps to establish himself as a contractor here in Gabriel Bend. While the legal stuff was being processed, he'd determined what needed to happen next at each building site and made calls to the subcontractors on Jay Graham's list. All this with the assumption that Holly wouldn't talk her partners into firing him before he even got started. She was the only one who had yet to sign the work contract he'd drawn up.

On Sunday morning, he made another weak excuse to his family about skipping church. He considered going out to the cabin to start the cleanup but couldn't find the motivation. This was supposed to be his and Davey's project, and he'd found himself counting on those hours with Holly's son entirely too much. Shadow had expressed his disappointment as well by giving Mark the stink eye all week.

Hearing his aunt and uncle returning from church, he heaved himself out of Uncle Hank's recliner and switched off the den TV, which he hadn't really been watching. Aunt Lois was a stickler for old-fashioned Sunday dinners with the family. She'd left him with instructions to put the roast in the oven at exactly ten forty-five and to peel and cube potatoes for boiling and mashing. He'd been asked to set the table, too, and hurried to the kitchen to look busy.

"Mmm, smells good in here," Lois said as Hank helped her slip off her coat. "Spencer and Lindsey are bringing Audra, so we'll need an extra place."

"On it." Mark took another plate from the cupboard, then rearranged the table settings to make room. Good thing it was a big country kitchen.

"Sunday dinners won't be the same without Arturo," Lois mused as she set a pot of water on to boil. "On the other hand, it's nice that Audra can finally join us. She was so patient and understanding about the whole Navarro-McClement feud business. I'm glad it's over and done with."

But was it? A twinge in Mark's belly brought to mind his mother's puzzling words: *"There remains more to*

be done here to put the past to rest, and my heart is tell-
ing me that task will fall to you."

With the arrival of Samuel, Joella and the baby, and
then Spencer and Lindsey with Audra, the kitchen became a hive of activity. Mark wasn't accustomed to
being around this many relatives, and though he'd always longed for the happy chaos of a big family, it reminded him too much of what he'd lost and would never
have.

After downing the obligatory slice of cherry pie for
dessert, he used Shadow's need to go outside as a reason to excuse himself.

"I'll join you." Spencer pushed back his chair.

They donned their jackets and strode out to the backyard. While Shadow sniffed around and took care of
business, Mark sank into an Adirondack chair. As he
inhaled a calming breath, an ashy smell from the cold
firepit wafted his way.

Spencer took the chair next to Mark's and leaned his
head back to look up at the sky. "I love my family, but
sometimes I just need a break."

"This is definitely going to take some getting used
to." Fingers laced over his full belly, Mark chuckled
softly. "Except I'm already getting spoiled by your
mom's cooking."

"If you think my mom's a great cook, you need to
come next door some evening when Holly's trying out
a new recipe. She fixed dinner for us on Thursday, and
I've never had shrimp and grits like she makes 'em."

Mark inched higher in his chair. Thursday evening…
when Shadow had gotten antsy, pestering Mark for the
walk he hadn't been in the mood for. If he'd let Shadow
out, the dog would probably have made a beeline for
next door to hang out with Davey.

And you would have had to go get your boy-obsessed dog and face the woman who's put your hard-won equilibrium on spin cycle.

Spencer released an appreciative groan. "Mom, Audra and Holly are planning a combined Navarro-McClement Thanksgiving feast this year, so I guarantee it'll be a meal to remember."

Mark had forgotten the holiday was only a few days away—rather, he'd tried to forget. Three years ago, Kellie had been battling hard to make it to one more Thanksgiving, her most favorite day of the year, but she'd passed away only hours before. "Afraid I'll have to miss it. I made other plans."

"Flying home to Montana to be with your folks?"

"No, I..." *Think fast, Caldwell.* "I thought I'd take Shadow on a little road trip, maybe to the coast. Can't remember the last time I was this close to a beach."

"Lindsey and I went to Galveston for our honeymoon. Aransas Pass is nice, too. Sure you want to spend Thanksgiving alone, though?"

Very sure. "It's been a weird couple of weeks. I could use the time away to clear my head."

"I hear you." Spencer sat up, one elbow on his knee as he shifted to face Mark. "I don't mean to pry, but... are you and God okay?"

A harsh laugh escaped Mark's throat. "Not in a long, long time."

"Thought that might be the case." Spencer gave a solemn nod. "Samuel drifted away from God for a while. You should talk to him."

"Why? So he can tell me how the Lord's going to make everything—" Squeezing his eyes shut, Mark swallowed the rest of the sentence. "Sorry, I know faith's a big deal in your family. But I lost mine when Kellie died."

"I didn't mean to push—"

"No worries." He rose abruptly and forced a smile. "Think I'll walk off that slab of pie I just ate. See you later."

Ever since Mark had taken them out to see the old cabin, Davey had been pestering Holly about going back, and she was running out of excuses. When she'd made supper last Thursday for everyone at the Mc-Clement ranch, she'd done most of the prep work in her own kitchen so there wouldn't be time to let Davey go next door.

The weekend had been the worst, though, with her boy chomping at the bit to escape their tiny apartment. Rather than deal with Mark, she'd invented a long list of chores and errands to keep them in town and suggested Davey make plans with one or two of his school friends. She'd tried really hard to write off Mark's snit as stress over recent developments in his life, but the man could be so infuriating!

She hadn't exactly been sorry to learn he'd mentioned a trip to the coast over Thanksgiving. Her son would be even more disappointed, but he'd have to get over it.

Problem was, Holly wasn't sure *she* could get over the confusing feelings Mark Caldwell evoked. Bad enough she'd had second thoughts about involving him in Davey's life. Now she faced being around him over the next few months while he completed the event center.

With Davey out of school for the Thanksgiving break, she'd made plans to spend Wednesday helping Audra with some advance cooking and baking. Her son was already pouting about Mark being out of town, and Holly could only hope the man had already left.

Unfortunately, he hadn't. Looking toward the Navarros' as she and Davey crossed Audra's backyard, she glimpsed Mark's big blue truck with the hood open. Mark, Spencer and Mr. Navarro were all poking around the engine while Samuel, the least mechanically minded of the group, stood nearby with his hands in his pockets.

"Mom, look, he's still here!" Davey tugged on her arm. "Can I go over there? Please?"

Arms loaded with grocery bags, she continued toward the house. "Looks like they're trying to get Mark's truck fixed so he can leave. You don't need to be bothering them."

"But can't I at least go over and tell him and Shadow goodbye? I haven't gotten to see them in over a week."

"I said no. Would you get the door for me, please?"

"Why do you always have to be so mean!" Stomping up the porch steps, Davey bumped her elbow and knocked one of the bags to the ground.

"Davey!" She gasped as whipping cream splattered the legs of her jeans and a bag of fresh cranberries split open.

He whirled around, eyes wide in panic. "Mom, I'm sorry!"

The back door swung open, and Lindsey came out. Her gaze dropped to the mess at the foot of the steps. "What happened?"

"We had a little accident." Riddled with guilt, Holly cast her son a regretful frown. If she hadn't been so stubborn about keeping him from spending time with Mark…

"I'll take care of this," Lindsey said, easing past. "Go on inside and clean yourself up."

Several minutes later, her pant legs damp but more presentable, Holly returned to the kitchen. Lindsey had made Davey a cup of hot chocolate, and Audra was sorting through the groceries Holly had brought.

Davey's red-rimmed eyes made it obvious he'd been fighting back tears. "I didn't mean to, Mom. Are you mad?"

"No, honey, just…frustrated. Mostly about grown-up stuff that I shouldn't have allowed to affect you." She tousled his wispy blond hair. "How about when you finish your cocoa, we go next door so you can see Mark and Shadow before they leave?"

"Really? Thanks, Mom!" Davey slurped faster.

Soon they were trekking across the field. Shadow saw them first and army-crawled under the barbed wire to greet Davey with yips and pirouettes. The dog's antics drew Mark's attention, and when his gaze met Holly's, he visibly stiffened.

By the time they ducked through the fence opening and reached the driveway, Mark had moved away from the men still working on the truck.

"Long time no see, kiddo." His welcoming grin for Davey couldn't disguise the uncertainty in his eyes as he glanced at Holly.

"Mom said you're going on a trip. Wish I could go with you."

Holly grimaced. "Davey…"

"Yeah, well…" Mark's eyebrow twitched. He rubbed it with a forefinger. "I might not be going anywhere for a while. My truck's broke."

Holly worked to keep her expression neutral. "Then I guess you'll be here for our big Thanksgiving feast after all."

"Guess so." Slanting a look toward Davey, already

rolling in the grass with Shadow, Mark softly cleared his throat. "Look, about the other day. I overreacted."

"We both seem to make a habit of that, don't we?"

"Yeah, what's the deal, huh?" He made a weak attempt at a laugh. "Anyway, I'm sorry. Especially if my loss of temper changed your mind about letting Davey hang out with me. Because he's a great kid, and I… I've missed him."

The desperately hopeful look in his eyes brought an ache to Holly's chest. "I happen to know the feeling is mutual—toward both you and Shadow." With a reluctant smile in Davey's direction, she added, "And the reason I know is because *I've* been in the doghouse for the past week."

Now Mark's laugh was genuine, and the sound of it warmed her heart. "I'd like the opportunity to change that, if it's okay with you," he murmured. "I hear you've got some cooking to do, so would you want to leave Davey with me for a few hours?"

"Are you sure? Because if you manage to get your truck running—"

"Pretty sure whatever's wrong is beyond our combined skills." He gestured toward his uncle and cousins, still examining the engine as if a solution would suddenly materialize. "With the long holiday weekend, not much chance of a garage repair before next week."

"That's too bad," she said, sincerely meaning it. "I'm sure you were looking forward to getting away for a few days."

"Another time, maybe. Besides, I want to be ready to start work on your building and Samuel's house first thing Monday."

She brightened. "Then you got all your arrangements taken care of?"

"All set. Jay Graham has been real helpful in connecting me with the right people."

"Hey, Mark!" Davey rushed over. "Have you been out to the old cabin again?"

"Only to spray for creepy-crawlies. Been waiting on the cleanup for you." With a hand clamped on Davey's shoulder, Mark cast Holly a questioning glance. When she nodded, he said, "I've had a slight change of plans—no trip this weekend. While your mom's busy cooking today, how about you and I take a picnic lunch out to the cabin and you can help me start fixing it up?"

Davey bounced on the toes of his sneakers. "Mom, can I?"

"As long as you stay right with Mark, mind whatever he tells you and don't go exploring by yourself."

"I promise!" Grinning from ear to ear, he threw his arms around Holly's waist. "Thanks, Mom!"

She staggered and caught her balance, laughing as her son took off to break the great news to Shadow. "Well, I think I'm officially out of the doghouse."

Mark tilted his head. With a cajoling tone, he asked, "Am I?"

How dare he be so exasperating one minute and so endearing the next? She forced a swallow. "For now." With the unexpected flutter of her heart betraying her, she took two giant steps backward. "Okay, then. I'll be next door. Cooking. If you need anything…"

"I have your cell phone number."

"Right. Of course you do." While she still maintained a semblance of composure, she spun around and headed for the gap in the fence.

"And don't worry," Mark called after her, though as fast as she took off, he couldn't be certain she'd heard.

At least they'd smoothed things over. Hopefully in the future, he could keep tighter control over his feelings. Although, considering the effect Holly Elliot and her son seemed to have on him, his emotional equilibrium was definitely in question.

He told the guys to give up on the truck, then went to the house to ask Aunt Lois for some lunch fixings. He stuffed his knapsack with ham sandwiches, chips, cookies, two apples and bottled water. That should tide them over for most of the day.

He filled a second tote with trash bags and a few cleaning supplies and borrowed one of Lois's old brooms. Davey took charge of the broom, which he wielded like a Jedi lightsaber as they made their way out to the cabin. Shadow played along in the role of a short, four-legged Wookiee.

The warm sunshine and mild November weather made ideal conditions for their day at the cabin. With Davey holding open a trash bag, Mark set to work sifting through the debris and tossing anything not worth salvaging. The one-room cabin held a few pieces of serviceable furniture, including a round wooden table and two chairs, an antique pie safe similar to what Mark remembered from his late Grandma Caldwell's house, and a wrought-iron double bed frame supporting a tattered mattress.

With most of the trash picked up, Davey grabbed the broom and began sweeping. Soon, the cloud of dust had them all sneezing, Shadow included.

Laughing between sneezes, Mark snatched the broom from Davey's hands. "That's enough for now. Let's let this place air out while we have some lunch."

Outside, they used one of the bottles of water to wash

their hands. Mark set out the food, and they sat on the porch step to eat.

Davey bit into his sandwich, then drew his shirtsleeve across his mouth. "Think we could sleep out here some night and go fishing like you said?"

"Maybe. It could get pretty cold after dark, though."

"But there's a potbelly stove."

"I'd have to check it out first. We wouldn't want to burn the place down."

"After you do, then." Davey nodded and took a swig of water.

Mark suppressed a grin. Even as hard as they'd been working, he hadn't had this much fun since…

Since before Kellie got so sick.

The stutter behind his breastbone made it difficult to swallow. His daughter would have liked Davey. Both had lively imaginations; both were stubbornly independent. If only Kellie'd had even a portion of Davey's boundless energy. Oh, what his precious girl could have accomplished if not for the lousy heart she'd been born with.

He drained his water bottle and shoved to his feet. "Ready to get back to work?"

Next, they tackled the contents of the pie safe. The shelves contained chipped dishes, dented cooking pans and an assortment of canned goods, much of which could have been there twenty years or more.

Davey inspected a rusty can of chili with a swollen lid. "Is this stuff still any good?"

"I wouldn't serve that to my worst enemy." Mark motioned toward the trash bag. "Let's toss all this old food."

Soon they'd emptied the cupboard, and he got busy wiping down the upper shelves while Davey worked on the lower ones. As Mark scrubbed grime near the farthest corner of the top shelf, he noticed something carved into the wood. He took out his phone and used the flashlight feature for a closer look.

It was a crude heart, most likely made with a pocket knife. Inside were the initials OM + AN.

A queasy sensation rolled through his belly. AN could stand for Alicia Navarro. His mother?

Then who was OM? A McClement, maybe? Beyond Audra and Lindsey, Mark didn't know much about the McClement family, but if his mother had once had a romantic relationship with one of them—and if Tito knew about it—that could explain a lot.

He tried not to dwell on his questions as he and Davey spent another hour or so on cleanup. Around three o'clock, he decided to call it a day. Hefting two bulging trash bags over one shoulder and with the tote of cleaning supplies in his other hand, he let Davey carry a lighter bag of trash and the mostly empty knapsack. After dropping everything off at the house, they went next door.

Audra's kitchen smelled like the inside of a five-star restaurant, with so many delicious aromas in the air that Mark's mouth watered—and Thanksgiving dinner wasn't until tomorrow.

Holly turned from the stove. "How'd it go?" Covering her nose with the back of her hand, she stifled a laugh. "Not that I even have to ask—you two are both *filthy*!"

"Sorry about that." Lips twitching, he stayed near the door. "We should have washed up before I brought Davey back."

Audra tossed her apron across the back of the chair. "Come upstairs with me, Davey. Let's see if we can scrape off a few layers."

Naturally, Shadow followed them.

Holly laid aside the long wooden spoon she'd been stirring with, then wet a handful of paper towels and handed them to Mark. "Here, this'll help a little."

The cool dampness felt good as he wiped his hands and face. "Wow. Whatever you're cooking smells amazing."

"I promise it tastes even better." Her smile brightened the whole room. "So good, in fact, that you might even decide your truck breaking down was a blessing in disguise."

He hated to admit it, but she could be right. Today with Davey had been a joy—except for his discovery in the pie safe, anyway. Frowning, he crumpled the dirty paper towels. "Is Spencer around?"

"Not right now. He and Lindsey rode out after lunch to do something with the cattle." She took the paper towels from him and dropped them in the trash.

"You've known Lindsey a long time, right?"

"Since high school." She returned to the stove and gave the pot a stir, releasing more of the enticing aroma.

"So I was wondering…" How could he ask his next question without inviting unwanted questions in return? "Living in Montana, I haven't gotten to see my cousins very often, and now that Spencer's married to Lindsey, I thought I should get to know the McClement side of the family a little better."

"That's nice. I'm sure they feel the same about you." She smiled over at him, then sampled a taste from the pot, her eyes closing in a thoughtful expression before she added a dash of something from a spice bottle.

He took a couple of steps closer, unsure whether it was the aroma that drew him or the woman at the stove. "You wouldn't know if someone in her family has a name beginning with *O*, would you?"

"Well, there's Owen, Lindsey's father." Holly shifted her glance between the front of the house and the back door, then lowered her voice. "But you probably shouldn't ask Lindsey or Audra about him. They aren't on good terms."

"I see."

She quirked a brow. "Was there some reason you wanted to know?"

"Uh, something I came across in the old cabin, that's all." The funny feeling in the pit of his stomach had returned. A couple of teenagers in love, a secluded shack with all the accoutrements for playing house…

Head tilted, she cast him a curious glance. "Mark, are you okay?"

"Yeah. Fine." *Not.*

Davey and Shadow returned to the kitchen just then. Drawing his hand across his mouth, Mark started for the door. "We should get out of your way. Come on, Shadow."

"Thanks so much for spending the day with Davey," Holly called out.

"Yeah, thanks, Mark," Davey added. "I had a total blast."

"It was fun for me, too. We'll do it again soon." He wished he could infuse more enthusiasm into his tone, but the recent direction his thoughts had taken didn't allow it. "See you tomorrow."

Without waiting for their goodbyes, he yanked the door closed behind him and trudged across the field with more questions than answers swirling through his brain.

Chapter Five

Holly was amazed. After only one full day in Mark's company, the change in her son's attitude was undeniable. Thanksgiving Day brought even more reason to rejoice. Davey didn't complain once when Holly had him ferrying food and tableware to and from Audra's dining room. Then, after dinner, he followed Mark's example by helping with the dishes—chores Holly struggled to get him to do at home, even with dire threats of completely cutting off his already closely monitored screen time.

On Saturday morning, Mark called to say Spencer would be giving him a combination horseback riding lesson and ranch tour that afternoon. "Think Davey'd like to come along?"

If Audra hadn't already been teaching her boy how to ride, Holly would be much less inclined to say yes. But with Spencer overseeing the outing, she trusted Davey would be well looked after. "He'd love it. What time?"

"How's one thirty sound?"

"He'll be there."

She'd just shared the news with Davey when Lindsey called. "I've talked Spencer into making this a family trail ride. Hank and Lois are riding with us, and Audra's watching Sophie so Samuel and Joella can go. Since Mark invited Davey, you should join us."

"Me? But I—"

"No excuses. You've been on a horse before."

Sorting laundry for the washer, she'd had the phone on speaker. Davey had overheard and tugged on her arm. "Come on, Mom. It'll be fun."

With both her best friend and her son urging her to go, she could hardly refuse. Shortly after one o'clock, she and Davey drove out to the McClement ranch.

Lindsey stood in front of the open barn door between two saddled horses. Inside, Spencer tightened the cinch on Ash, the gentle gray gelding Davey had been learning on. One of Spencer's rescues, Ash had endeared himself so much to them that he and Lindsey had decided to adopt him themselves.

"Hank will have a horse for you next door," Lindsey said, adding with a wink, "I told him to pick out the laziest one he could find."

With a pretend scowl, Holly followed Davey into the barn to remind him to get his riding helmet from the tack room. Better safe than sorry, she found an extra for herself. While the others mounted and headed to the Navarro ranch via the road, Holly cut across the field to the opening in the fence.

Hearing sounds in the main barn, she found Mark sitting astride a tall palomino while Hank Navarro adjusted the stirrups. Mark looked anything but relaxed, his gaze shifting beneath the black brim of a riding helmet.

As Holly approached, he offered a tense smile. "Greenhorn alert."

"Makes two of us," she said. "I have no idea what possessed me to agree to this."

"You didn't want me to make a fool of myself alone?"

Hank laughed as he finished adjusting Mark's stirrups. "You'll both do fine. Holly, I've got a sweet little mare already saddled for you. Come with me."

Helmet buckled, she allowed Hank to give her a leg up, then settled into a cushy suede saddle with padding in all the right places. Maybe this wouldn't be so bad after all.

Holly, Mark and Davey joined Spencer in the arena for a few quick horseback riding pointers, and then everyone headed out. Naturally, the married couples paired off, which left Holly riding next to Mark. Davey rode in front of them, with Shadow trotting alongside.

Glancing forward and back, she noted they were sandwiched between Lindsey and Spencer in the lead and Hank and Lois following behind, with Samuel and Joella bringing up the rear. "Looks like we've been strategically placed between the most experienced riders."

"Works for me." Mark kept one hand firmly clamped on the saddle horn.

They meandered along a dirt lane, which Holly recognized from the day Mark had taken her and Davey out to the old cabin. Several minutes later, she spotted it in the distance. Davey pointed and called, "Hey, Mark, when can we go back?"

"Not sure." Adam's apple working, he stared straight ahead.

Did his curt reply have to do with feeling ill at ease on a horse, or was something else bothering him? Holly's thoughts whirled back to Wednesday, when he'd returned Davey after their workday at the cabin. Something had been off about Mark then, too. And his curiosity about Lindsey's father—what was that about?

Beyond the cabin, they veered from the lane and across an unfenced field. Spencer brought the group to a halt, then turned his horse to face them. He gestured over his shoulder. "Just beyond those trees and the river is the southwestern edge of our property. Then the river bends around to the northwest past the McClement ranch."

Mark surveyed the rocky, rolling stretch of land. "What's this part of the ranch used for?"

"Nothing these days." Spencer looked past them toward his parents. "Dad, didn't you tell me they used to graze cattle back here before Tito broke ties with the McClements?"

Hank rode up on Holly's other side. "That's what I recall. But ever since we became strictly a horse ranch, this area's been left alone. Partly because of the rough terrain, but mostly because it's so far out of the way."

They continued riding, following the tree line. Through breaks in the vegetation, Holly caught glimpses of the sun reflecting off the water. The burbling of the gently flowing river evoked a sense of peace. "It's beautiful out here," she said with a sigh. "Feels like a million miles from the city."

"I hope we can keep it this way." Grimacing, Hank shook his head. "But the next town over keeps growing. In ten or twenty years, we'll likely have developers hounding us to sell off some of this acreage. I hate to think what all that development will do to the river."

"Audra's mentioned her concerns, too," Lindsey said. They'd reached the barbed-wire fence dividing the two ranches, where it ended at the riverbank. Reining her horse to a halt, she swept the area with a wistful gaze.

"Hard to believe all this used to be one big ranch. Wish I could have seen it back in its heyday."

As they headed in the direction of the barn, Holly became aware of Mark's lengthy silence. His serious manner suggested something heavy weighed on his mind. Perhaps the fact that now a portion of the land they'd just ridden through would belong to him? Provided he stayed for the full year, of course.

But *would* he? He didn't appear quite as uncomfortable on horseback as when they'd first started out, but a family trail ride was a far cry from stepping fully into the business of raising and training horses. Once the event center and Joella and Samuel's house were complete, would he find strong enough motivation to keep him in Texas? Or would he give all this up and return to Montana?

Ever since they'd passed the old cabin, Mark's mother's words had been echoing through his mind, growing even more insistent as they'd neared the barbed-wire fence *"...put the past to rest...that task will fall to you."*

The rocky land on the McClement side continued the stretch of wild, rambling scenery dotted with cedars, live oaks, mesquite and cacti. It held a different kind of appeal than the mountains around Missoula, but it was impressive nonetheless. Easy to imagine how a couple of eager young army buddies would have seen nothing but opportunity here.

What could his mother have meant, though? It wasn't as if he could change the fact that Arturo Navarro and Egan McClement had gone from best friends to bitter enemies. Besides, Tito's passing had brought an end to that generation, and the surviving Navarros and McClements seemed to be getting along fine these days.

Wasn't it now merely a matter of leaving the past behind and moving on?

At the barn, Mark climbed from the saddle and turned his horse over to one of the stable hands, then helped Holly dismount. Davey rode back to the McClement ranch with Spencer and Lindsey, and when Shadow decided to accompany them, Mark could only shake his head. The dog would find his way home in time for supper if not before. Aunt Lois went to the house and Uncle Hank took off toward one of the pastures, leaving Mark and Holly alone outside the barn.

"I'll be feeling this tomorrow." Holly gave her lower back a good stretch. "Gorgeous scenery, but I had no idea your ranch was so big."

"Can't claim any part of it as mine yet." *If ever.*

"I just meant—"

"It's okay." Taking a few steps to the side, Mark gazed out across the pastures. "Today was an eye-opener for me, too."

Holly looped her helmet straps over her arm as she came up beside him. "You did seem awfully preoccupied this afternoon. I can be a pretty good listener—I mean, if it would help to talk with someone who isn't family…"

He made the mistake of looking down into those mesmerizing eyes, and his breath caught at the base of his throat. He released a quiet cough. "That's a kind offer."

"Well, I've bent your ear too many times already about my problems. So if I can return the favor—"

"You wouldn't want to go somewhere for coffee, would you?" *Did I really just say that?*

Mouth gaping, she looked equally surprised. "Did you mean now, or…"

"I guess it is kind of last-minute." He dragged his fingers through his hair. "You probably have other things to do."

Before she could reply, Audra came down from Samuel and Joella's apartment. "Hey, you two. Heard y'all had a good ride."

"We did," Holly said. "Sorry you couldn't come along."

"I spend plenty of time on horseback as it is. My afternoon with Sophie was delightful." As Audra shifted her gaze between them, a perceptive smile quirked her lips. "Holly, if you're not in a hurry to get Davey home, I'll be happy to keep an eye on him for a bit."

"Now that you mention it, I was thinking about… running an errand in town." She cast Mark a quick glance. "Actually, the both of us were. But I wouldn't be gone long."

"Take as much time as you need." Audra winked. "I'm making turkey noodle soup with Thanksgiving leftovers for supper. We can eat whenever you get back. You're welcome to join us, too, Mark."

"Thanks, but, uh…"

"Maybe another time, then. Y'all have fun in town." Giving a jaunty wave, Audra started toward the fence.

Mark typically considered himself a closed book, but apparently the women around here—two of them, anyway—could read him like the dictionary. Sucking air through his teeth, he turned to Holly. "So does this mean we're going for coffee?"

"Guess so." She gave her jeans a quick swipe with her hand. "As long as it's someplace where they don't mind the smell of horses."

"In a ranching town like Gabriel Bend, I figure that'd be just about anywhere."

With his truck still out of commission, he asked to borrow Aunt Lois's compact sedan. Even with the seat cranked all the way back, he felt like his knees were up to his ears.

Holly snickered from the passenger seat. "Maybe we should have taken my minivan."

"Too late now." He laughed with her, and for reasons he couldn't explain, it felt good. "But I hope you brought a can opener to get me out of this thing later."

As they neared downtown, he asked for Holly's suggestions for a quiet place to talk.

"Bonnie's Bistro shouldn't be too busy yet. And they have great pie."

"What—you didn't get enough pie on Thanksgiving?"

She wiggled her brows. "It's always a treat when someone else does the cooking *and* the cleanup."

No arguing that point. He found a parking spot across the street from the café. By the time he'd extricated himself from the car, Holly was waiting for him on the curb—and doing a very poor job of hiding her amusement.

"Wish I'd recorded that," she said with a muffled laugh. "We could have won the ten-thousand-dollar prize on *America's Funniest Home Videos.*"

He tried looking offended, but it was no use. *Admit it, she's starting to get under your skin.*

At Bonnie's, Mark chose a booth in the far corner, where red gingham curtains parted on a view of the street. Holly decided on blackberry cobbler à la mode and decaf, and Mark opted for the same. After the server returned with their orders, they spent the next few minutes savoring their desserts with occasional murmurs of satisfaction.

"I can see why you like this place," he said as he scraped the last traces of melted ice cream and blackberry filling from the sides of his bowl.

Holly licked her spoon, then laid it aside and folded her arms along the edge of the table. "Have we stalled long enough yet?"

Mark winced. He'd all but forgotten why he'd asked her to come to town with him. Or else he'd purposely tried to push it from his mind. He wrapped his hands around his mug and focused on the inch or so of decaf in the bottom. "Maybe this wasn't such a good idea."

She was quiet for so long that he finally had to glance up. He found her patiently looking at him, lips slanted in a concerned frown. "If you don't feel like talking, we can go."

"No, you were right. I could use another perspective. Like you said, from someone who isn't family."

"Okay, then. Why don't you start at the beginning?"

A sharp laugh escaped. "I'm not sure exactly where that is." The server came by to refill their mugs, which gave him a moment to frame his next words. When they were alone again, he said, "Remember the other day when I asked you about Owen McClement?"

"Yes."

He pressed his index fingers above his closed eyes. After a moment, he straightened and hauled in a breath, then described the carved initials he'd discovered in the pie safe. "I think maybe Owen and my mother had something going on."

Once more, Holly remained silent. She sat stiffly, her lips pressed together as she stared out the window. "You're right, they did. I don't know all the details, but Lindsey told me it's why her parents divorced and why her father turned his back on the McClement ranch."

Blackberry cobbler sat like a stone in the pit of Mark's stomach. "Can you tell me what you do know?"

"I'm not sure I should. It isn't my place..."

"Please. I can't ask my mother—not yet, anyway—and I don't want to upset Lindsey or Audra."

Holly studied him, brows bunching as comprehension dawned. "Oh, no. You don't think..."

"I don't know *what* to think. But things are starting to add up. Things I never questioned as a kid and had no reason to as an adult." He released a sardonic laugh. "I knew from my birth certificate that I was born only six months after my parents got married. But my parents love each other—always have, as far as I know. Why would I think my mother had been involved with anyone besides my dad?"

Holly reached across the table to grasp his hand. "Don't jump to conclusions. Just because your mom and Lindsey's dad snuck away to the cabin for a teenage tryst doesn't mean they—" Her face reddened. She withdrew her hand and tucked it in her lap.

Mark scoffed. "Two lovesick teens alone in a deserted cabin? Yeah, what are the odds?"

"Even so..." Looking away, Holly shook her head. Clearly, the possibility that Owen McClement could be his father was as hard for her to deny as it was for him.

Shoving away from the table, he snatched the ticket their server had left. "I shouldn't have involved you in this. I'll take you back to the ranch."

While Mark went to the counter to pay, Holly stepped out to the sidewalk. Hands stuffed into her jacket pockets, she tried to imagine his turmoil. What must it be like after all these years to discover the man who'd raised him might not be his real father?

And how could he go about proving or disproving his suspicions without risking distress for a whole lot of people he cared about? Only after the fact had Samuel and Joella revealed their private worries over the possibility that Samuel's former girlfriend had lied and Sophie wasn't really his baby. It had taken a DNA test to settle the paternity question once and for all.

What ever happened to the typical two-parent family with 2.5 kids living happily ever after in suburbia? It was a myth, of course. An impossible ideal. Marriages ended, families blended, relationships continually changed or rearranged for better or for worse. All anyone could hope for was to accept and adjust.

Mark joined Holly on the sidewalk. Studying her, he frowned. "I ruined the rest of your day, didn't I?"

"You got me thinking, that's all." As they started walking, she attempted a smile, but it faded into a lengthy sigh. "Life never quite goes as planned."

"No kidding."

"I try hard not to question God, but I do wonder why He lets some things happen…or doesn't."

"I quit asking after Kellie got so sick. Got tired of waiting for answers that never came."

They'd reached the corner, and as they entered the crosswalk, Mark lightly touched Holly's elbow. The protective gesture reminded her of Blaine, and somehow it felt…right.

She cast him a grateful smile. "For months after my husband died, I lost any sense of God's presence. But Davey needed me, and faith has always been my only true source of strength, so I pressed into God as hard as I could."

"And did it work for you?" Mark sounded both skeptical and hopeful.

"It took time, but yes." They stepped onto the opposite curb and continued toward the car. "I experienced God's comfort through loving friends and family. When I needed to find a way to make a living, I sensed His direction to start a home-based catering service. And I especially felt His nudge when Lindsey and Joella asked me to move here and be part of River Bend Events."

Halting in front of a papered-over storefront window, Mark faced her. "So…you believe God brought you here? That He had this particular path in mind for you all along?"

"You mean was Gabriel Bend always His plan for Davey and me? The Bible says God's ways and thoughts are higher than ours, so I won't pretend to read His mind. But I…" She peered around him, her attention captured by a faded design on the window glass of the vacant shop. The hand-painted nosegays tied with curling blue ribbons evoked memories that made her heart trip. "I, um…"

"Something wrong?"

"Those flowers…they reminded me of something." She gave herself a quick mental shake. "I'm sorry—what were we talking about?"

"Never mind. It's not important." He did a terrible job of hiding a grimace. "Tell me about the flowers."

"From my third birthday on, every year until she died, my grandmother would treat my mom and me to a lovely lunch at her favorite ladies' tearoom. I remember the menu was decorated with little bouquets and trailing ribbons very much like these." She stepped closer, lightly touching the design on the window. "I still miss those special times. I miss Gran even more. She lost her battle with cancer shortly before my eleventh birthday."

His expression softened. "That must have been hard."

"Yeah, it was. But Gran and those birthday lunches instilled my love of cooking. And more than just cooking, but creating an occasion. Since food is essential for life, why not make it memorable?"

Mark scuffed the back of his head. "Never thought of it that way. When I get hungry, I eat."

"Why am I not surprised?" A snicker escaped Holly's throat. The man had his idiosyncrasies, but he was proving to be much more likable than first impressions suggested.

Turning toward the shop window again, she hugged herself as another wave of melancholy swept over her. "I was always going to open my own tearoom someday," she murmured. "Until life happened."

"Funny how that works." Mark nodded toward the car. "Ready to head back?"

"Yes, Davey must be wondering what's keeping me."

He opened the passenger door for her, then folded himself behind the steering wheel. The sight of him maneuvering his big, muscular frame into a space clearly designed for a smaller driver elicited another chuckle. "I really should get that on video."

"You really should *not*." He shot her a pointed look—and a grin—that made her stomach flip.

Deciding it was wiser to keep her eyes straight ahead, she abruptly faced forward. Shortly, they were on the road out of town.

After a few minutes of silence, Mark asked, "So what's keeping you from opening your own tearoom?"

Now she couldn't avoid looking his way, this time with a disbelieving stare. "Only an inconsequential little thing called money."

"But couldn't you get a small business loan, maybe a grant of some kind?"

"I'm already committed up to my eyebrows with River Bend Events." Shoulders heaving, she shifted her gaze to the side window as oaks and cedars and fence posts whizzed by. "Besides, I have Davey to think about. Opening and managing my own restaurant would require huge amounts of both time and energy."

Mark drove another mile or so without saying anything. "You made it sound like something you really wanted to do, that's all."

Her throat tightened. "Wanting something and having it are two entirely different things."

What was it about this woman that made her happiness so important to him? First he'd let himself be talked into building the event center, then he'd agreed to be her son's mentor. Now, of all things, Mark found himself earnestly wanting her to have the fancy ladies' tearoom that seemed to mean so much to her. What was supposed to be a straightforward and therefore *brief* trip to Texas for his grandfather's funeral had rapidly become a major life changer.

He steered the car up the McClements' driveway and stopped beside the house. What should he do now? Tell her he had a nice time? Except confiding in her about his complicated family issues didn't exactly constitute a date. He should just thank her for lending an ear and say goodbye.

"I appreciate—" he began.

"This was nice," she said at the same time.

They both gave embarrassed laughs. He flicked his hand. "Ladies first."

"Okay. Thank you for the pie and coffee. It's been a while since I…since…" She lowered her chin and glanced away.

"Yeah. Me, too." His Adam's apple felt more like an overripe McIntosh. "I just wanted to say I appreciate you being an objective listener."

"Of course, I'll keep everything you told me in strictest confidence. Also… I'd rather you didn't mention the tearoom to anyone. I've never talked about it before. It's always been my secret dream." She gave a self-deprecating laugh. "And I have *no* earthly idea why I mentioned it to you."

"Guess we were both in need of a confidant."

"Guess so." She reached for the door handle. "Oh, Audra did invite you for supper. Will you change your mind and stay?"

"I'd better pass. I have some thinking to do."

With an understanding smile, she stepped from the car. She hesitated in the open door, then leaned in. "Then how about you join Davey and me for dinner at our place one evening next week?" She cast him a persuasive grin. "I promise to cook something *memorable* for you."

Holly Elliot was getting too close for comfort, and every common-sense instinct in his body told him he should politely refuse. "I look forward to it."

Did his mouth have absolutely zero connection to his brain?

"Great." She looked toward the house. "Before you go, should we check if Shadow's still over here with Davey?"

"That's okay. If they're having fun, send him next door when you leave." By then, surely the dog would be ready to come home for supper—unless Davey'd been practicing tricks with Shadow and filling him up with cheese sticks.

"Well, thanks again for the pie and coffee." Warmth

radiated from those captivating green eyes. "And, Mark?"

"Yeah?"

"Wherever your discovery leads, I'll be praying for you. And your family."

Her words burrowed beneath the wall around his heart and lodged deep. Was he anywhere close to letting God in again? If his parents hadn't been able to sway him, why should Holly be any different?

He managed a weak nod of thanks and said he'd better be going.

Yep, things in his life were changing faster than he could keep up. If he had any hope of surviving the next year, it might just take an act of God.

Chapter Six

Over the next week, Mark began putting crews back to work on both the event center and Samuel's house. It did feel good to be managing construction jobs again. He'd left things open-ended with Bob in Montana, saying they could talk about what to do with the business up there once Mark decided whether he'd be staying in Gabriel Bend long-term.

During the day, he had little time to think much about his mother and Owen McClement, but while he tossed and turned between midnight and dawn most nights, the ramifications weighed heavily. If he really was Owen's biological son, did Dad know?

Dad. No matter what, David Caldwell would always be Mark's father—his *only* father. The bits and pieces he'd gleaned about Owen didn't make him sound like a parent anyone would want to claim.

Early Friday afternoon, as Mark supervised the framing carpenters working on the event center, he glimpsed Holly crossing the driveway. Remaining a safe distance away, she waved and called to him over the *pop-pop* of nail guns. "Got a minute?"

He strode over. Tucking his helmet beneath his arm

and finger-combing his hair, he wondered when he'd been quite this self-conscious about his appearance at a construction site. "What can I do for you?"

"The days got away from me, and obviously you've been busy." She gestured toward the framers, looking suddenly shy. "And here it is Friday and I never got back to you about coming over for dinner."

He'd almost forgotten, too. Not to mention he'd neglected his mentoring duties. "Sorry I haven't been available to spend time with Davey after school. Once these jobs get rolling, I should have a little more flexibility." He snorted. "Shadow hasn't been real happy with me, either."

"I noticed I haven't seen him around as much."

"Bringing him to a job site isn't safe. Aunt Lois has been keeping him in the house during the day."

"Probably wise." She tucked her fingers into her sweater pockets. "So…are you free this evening? I did promise to cook for you, and you and Davey could catch up."

"That'd be nice. I've missed him." Only then did he realize how much.

"And bring Shadow, of course."

Mark laughed. "Like he'd let me out the door without him if he knew where I was headed."

"Great. I'm on my way to get Davey from school and make a supermarket run. What time will you finish work for the day?"

"Fiveish. But I'll need a half hour or so to clean up."

"Then I'll plan dinner for six thirty, but come whenever you're ready. I'll text you my address."

The next three-plus hours crawled by. How long had it been since Mark had felt this kind of anticipation? How long since he'd felt much of *anything*?

Shortly after four thirty, he told the crew to stow their tools and secure the site. Wishing them a good weekend, he climbed into his truck—running again, as of Tuesday—and made the short trip down the road to do the same with the workers at Samuel's house. Within the hour, he'd changed into a nubby beige pullover and a clean pair of jeans. He fed Shadow his supper, and shortly they were on the way to town with the dog riding shotgun.

Gabriel Bend was small enough that he had no trouble finding Holly's place, an apartment over someone's garage. The neighborhood was typical of what Mark had observed in the Texas Hill Country—houses sided with brick or Austin stone, and a fairly even mix of grassy lawns and hardscape.

A pair of floodlights cast a yellow glow across the driveway and side yard. He'd no sooner parked than Davey tore down the stairs beside the garage and ran up to the truck. With Shadow scratching at the window and yipping loud enough to pierce Mark's eardrums, he let the dog out before he did any damage—to his ears or the truck door.

"Yay, you're here!" Davey knelt and patted his knees, and Shadow leaped into his arms, tongue going a mile a minute.

Mark stepped from the truck. "What am I, chopped liver?"

"Hi, Mark." Davey stood, his attempt to look contrite not quite cutting it. "Mom's upstairs cooking. Can I play with Shadow out here till dinner's ready?"

"Fine with me if your mom doesn't mind." He watched them for a moment before heading up.

Through the door glass, Mark glimpsed Holly checking something in the oven. He rapped lightly. Hands ensconced in oven mitts, she smiled and motioned for him to come in.

Delicious aromas greeted him. "Mmm, smells good. What is it?"

"My version of Tex-Mex shepherd's pie." She tossed the oven mitts onto the counter, then whisked a lock of hair off her forehead. "I hope you don't mind a little spice."

"My mother's Latina, remember? I think I can handle it."

Holly poured two glasses of iced tea, then gestured toward the sitting area. "We have a few minutes. Take off your jacket and make yourself comfortable."

Guessing the Scandinavian-style blue chair and ottoman would be Holly's preference, Mark squeezed past and chose the beige sofa. The narrow space didn't have room for much else besides a TV and combination entertainment center/bookcase.

"It's cramped, I know." She lowered herself onto the blue chair and set her glass on the triangle-shaped end table between her and Mark. "When we moved here, I had to put most of our things in storage. Someday I hope we can afford something bigger."

The sad tilt to those beautiful green eyes tugged at Mark's heart. "Yeah, a growing boy needs space."

"At least my landlord doesn't mind Davey playing in the backyard." She glanced toward the window, where the boy's muted laughter filtered in. "Thank you for bringing Shadow. Sounds like they're having a great time down there."

"Mmm-hmm."

Awkwardness began to set in. Mark let his gaze roam the bookshelves. One shelf held nothing but cookbooks, some so tattered that the spines had split. Framed photos lined another shelf—Holly with hair almost to her waist, an average-looking blond guy with glasses, several of Davey at different ages and a studio portrait with all three of them together. Davey couldn't have been more than four or five in that one.

Unable to resist, Mark crossed to the bookcase for a closer look. He indicated the studio portrait. "Your husband?"

"Yes. Blaine." Her voice softened with nostalgia. "That was taken for the church pictorial directory a year before he…he was killed."

"Blaine," he repeated under his breath. He touched another photo, then turned to Holly. "When did you cut your hair?"

Color rose in her cheeks. She pressed a hand to her shoulder-length brown waves. "A few years ago. It got to be too much trouble." Jumping up, she barely missed knocking over her iced tea glass. "I'd better check on dinner. Want to go spend a little time with Davey?"

"Okay, sure." He retrieved his jacket from the end of the sofa and started for the door.

Great. He'd managed to make Holly as uncomfortable as he was. Maybe accepting her invitation hadn't been such a smart idea.

Holly hadn't given a single thought to how it would feel having Mark see—much less comment on—her treasured family photos. Blaine had loved her long hair. She couldn't tell Mark she'd whacked it off with kitchen scissors less than a month after Blaine's death. At her mother's urging, she'd eventually let a stylist turn the cut into something more presentable. Changing her appearance had seemed a necessary step toward accepting herself as an individual instead of half a couple.

Which explained why, four years later, she found it so hard to make room for another man in her life. Not that she thought of Mark *that way*. But he did stir feelings she'd thought were buried with her late husband.

After another check of the shepherd's pie, she gave the table settings a once-over, then wandered to the bookcase. Fingering the array of photos, she selected the one Blaine had snapped the day they'd gone looking for the tearoom where her grandmother used to take her. They'd discovered the restaurant had closed years before and an upscale coffee shop had moved in. Blaine had captured Holly with her back to the camera, her longing expression reflected in the window as the breeze toyed with her hair.

Now, she glimpsed her reflection in the frame glass. How strange to see her present-day self superimposed upon the woman she used to be.

And she definitely was *not* the same person. As a young wife and mother, she'd believed herself all grown up. Little had she known how much more growing she still had to do. She'd recently turned thirty-one, but a mature, got-it-mostly-all-together adult? Not even close.

Footsteps sounded on the stairs outside. The door flew open, and Davey bounded in, Shadow right beside him and Mark a few paces behind. Clumps of dry grass shimmied from her son's clothes onto the floor, but he looked so happy and pleasantly out of breath that Holly couldn't bring herself to scold him.

A moment later, the oven timer dinged. She silenced it and donned her oven mitts. "Go wash up, you two. Dinner is served."

When they sat down to eat, with Mark wedged into a chair between the counter and the table, Holly's tiny kitchen felt even smaller. He didn't seem to notice, though, instead raving about her "incredible" shepherd's pie. She'd made extra, so after they finished, she transferred half the leftovers into a plastic container to send home with him.

She tried to refuse his help with the dishes, but he insisted. His masculine presence beside her at the sink made it hard to catch a breath. As she handed him the last plate to dry, their fingers brushed, sending a zing up her arm. If Mark hadn't caught the dish, it surely would have shattered on the tile floor.

"Well, I think that's it," Holly said, noting the telltale squeak in her voice. She drained the sink and rinsed out the dishcloth, then dried her hands. "Thanks for your help."

"Thank *you* for the meal. And for the leftovers." Mark picked up the container and started toward the sitting area. He halted abruptly and shook his head. "I think they're down for the count."

Holly tiptoed over to find Davey and Shadow snuggled close on the area rug in front of the sofa, both of them sound asleep. She pressed a hand to her heart. "Davey's made a friend for life."

Mark sighed. "I almost hate to wake Shadow to take him home."

"And somehow I'll have to get Davey into his pajamas and tucked in bed."

"Or…" One brow hiked, he looked down at her. "Will you be coming out to the ranch in the morning?"

"Yes, we were planning another workday to get ready for a couple of holiday events." Holly frowned as his meaning registered. "You'd leave Shadow here overnight?"

He nodded toward the boy and dog. "They'd both be a lot happier, don't you think?"

"You may be right, but…" The note of melancholy in his tone hadn't escaped her. "What about you?"

He scoffed. "I think I can handle one night without a hairy mutt hogging half the bed."

"Well, if you're sure. We should be out around eight thirty or nine tomorrow. Can Shadow wait till then for his breakfast?"

"As long as he has Davey to distract him, he'll be fine." Giving a rough clear of his throat, Mark reached past her for his jacket. "I'll be going, then. Thanks again for dinner."

When he'd left, Holly slipped into Davey's room and brought out his pillow and comforter. Kneeling, she eased the pillow beneath her son's head, then spread the comforter over both boy and dog. No reason they couldn't snuggle on the floor for a bit until she could rouse her son enough to get him into his own bed. Shadow slitted one eye briefly, then nestled closer to Davey and released a contented doggy sigh.

Heaving a sigh of her own, Holly kicked off her shoes and scooted onto the sofa. With her knees drawn up and her head resting on a throw pillow, she let the day's tension seep from her limbs. She breathed in and caught a woodsy smell, with hints of leather and lime…

Mark's jacket had been lying across this pillow.

Her heart gave a disconcerting shudder, and she bolted upright with a gasp. This evening had been nice—*too* nice. Mark was Davey's mentor and their building contractor. She couldn't let her loneliness become a longing for anything more.

Arriving at the McClement ranch the next morning, Holly sent Davey next door to return Shadow. A few minutes later, Mark texted asking if Davey could go with him to the cabin for more cleanup and a picnic lunch.

She imagined her son with puppy-dog eyes to rival Shadow's and whisper-pleading, "Can I, Mom? Please, please, please?"

Replying with her consent, she sent up a silent prayer: *Lord, don't You dare let Mark break my little boy's heart.*

After spending the morning arranging a high school band banquet and adding finishing touches to plans for the Gracey-Totten wedding, Holly welcomed a break. Audra called them to the kitchen for tomato soup and grilled cheese sandwiches.

Joella swallowed a bite of sandwich. "I can't believe how much Mark has accomplished in barely a week. The framers are practically finished at our house."

"It's wonderful to see progress again," Lindsey agreed. "Our event center just might be completed on schedule after all."

Shortly, Spencer came in, and while he washed up, Lindsey grilled a sandwich for him and filled a soup bowl. When he joined them at the table, he mentioned seeing Mark and Davey on their way back from the cabin.

"Already?" Holly hadn't expected them to return so soon. She tilted her bowl to scoop the last spoonful of soup, then carried her dishes to the sink. "If we're done for the day, I should head over and get Davey."

With no arguments from her friends, she gathered her things and drove to the Navarros'. Parking in the driveway, she spotted her son absently tossing the ball for Shadow in the backyard. "Hey, hon," she said, striding over. "Where's Mark?"

"On the phone. He sounds mad."

Mark's raised voice reached her from between the arena and barn. She couldn't hear everything he was saying—mainly the words *Mom* and *cabin*—and he definitely seemed upset.

Her stomach knotted. Casting a worried look in Mark's direction, she reached for Davey's hand. "Honey, I think we should go."

"But shouldn't you find out what's wrong? Maybe Mark needs help."

"He'd probably rather—"

Mark came toward them, his knuckles white on the cell phone gripped at his side. "Sorry, I…" Adam's apple working, he jammed his fingers through his hair. "My mom called as we were heading back, and I couldn't help it. I had to ask."

His stricken look revealed the gist of their conversation. "Oh, Mark."

He shot a glance at Davey, then lowered his voice. "I'd tell you more, but…"

Holly nodded. Turning to her son, she said brightly, "Hey, Davey, can you keep Shadow company for a few minutes? Mark and I are going to sit in the van and talk."

Concern filled her son's perceptive frown as he knelt to pat Shadow's head. "It'll be okay, Mark. My mom's the best at making bad stuff better."

Heart twisting, she blinked back a sudden tear. After all their squabbles lately, her little boy actually thought that?

Recovering her composure, she climbed in behind the wheel while Mark strode around to the passenger side.

He slumped into the seat, his chin dropping to his chest. "She admitted it. Owen McClement is my biological father." As he looked toward the side window, a low moan rose in his throat. "I don't even know who I am anymore. A Navarro? A McClement? Definitely not a Caldwell."

"Is the name so important? You're still you." Then another question filled her mind. "Your father—David—does he know?"

"Yep, he's known all along." Bitterness laced Mark's tone. "Thirty-nine years later, and they never felt like I deserved the truth."

"They must have had their reasons." Although Holly couldn't immediately come up with anything that made sense.

"It had everything to do with the feud, apparently. My grandfather couldn't stomach the idea of his daughter involved with a McClement, much less having his baby. So Tito quietly shipped her off to Colorado to live with an aunt." Mark huffed. "Now I get why the cabin is all Mom got in the will."

The unresolved rift between father and daughter saddened Holly as she mentally put the pieces together. "Your mother must have met your father pretty quickly after that."

"The aunt's best friend had a son a couple years older than Mom. It was basically an arranged marriage for the sake of propriety, with an agreement that if he wanted out after I was born, he'd be free to leave with no obligation to my mother or to me."

The terms sounded cold and manipulative. "But I met your parents last spring at your grandfather's birthday celebration. I saw how they looked at each other...how they looked at *you*." The memory squeezed her heart. "No one can fake that depth of love."

Fists clenched against his thighs, Mark exhaled

slowly. "I've never doubted my parents' love, for each other or for me. But now…"

"Now you're confused and hurt." Instinctively, Holly laid her hand atop Mark's. "You shouldn't have had to find out this way, but you also can't change what happened or the decisions that were made. Unless you find a way to forgive your parents—forgive your grandfather—blame and resentment will destroy you. Give it to God. He can handle it."

He turned his hand over, his fingers lacing through hers as he lifted his gaze. "Is that what you did to get past losing your husband—give it all over to God? Because it sure didn't work for me when Kellie died."

She heard no condemnation in his tone, only a desperate need to understand. "I didn't mean for it to sound so easy, because it wasn't. Still isn't. But knowing God cares, that He's always with me, even in the pain, and even when I can't feel His presence—it's where I find the strength to face each day. It's how I find gratitude for the good in my life right now."

He nodded as if mulling over her words. "Seems I've lost sight of the good things. Before my folks went home to Montana, my dad basically told me I haven't really been living, just going through the motions." A sigh escaped. "He's more right than I want to admit."

"Hmm, sounds like something else to include in your next conversation with God."

He lifted a brow. "You're assuming there'll be one."

"I'm assuming you're smart enough to give Him another chance."

"Smart enough…or desperate enough?" The gentle pressure of his fingers entwined with hers increased. "Davey's right—you're pretty good at making the bad stuff better."

Heat singed her cheeks. She freed her hand and tucked it into her lap. "Now that you know the truth about Owen—what will you do?"

"Break it to the rest of the family, I guess. They have a right to know, too." He clenched his jaw. "I'm barely getting acquainted with Lindsey. How's she gonna handle learning I'm her half brother?"

"Probably not well at first, but she and Audra will both realize none of this is your fault. And think of it this way…now you'll have *two* extended families who care about you."

Nervous laughter rumbled from him. "Scary thought." He straightened and reached for the door handle. "You probably want to get going. Thanks for letting me bend your ear, and for the advice."

"I'll keep praying for you." She pondered inviting him to church with her and Davey in the morning, but since she belonged to the same church as Audra, Lindsey and Spencer, it probably wasn't the best idea, at least for now.

As he stepped from the van, she asked him to send Davey over. It took her son another five minutes to finish saying his goodbyes to Shadow, and then he said something to Mark and gave him a big hug. When Mark bent down to plant a fatherly kiss on Davey's head, Holly's heart lurched.

Oh, how her son had needed this relationship!

And maybe you do, too?

Chapter Seven

Later Saturday afternoon, Mark had a lengthy phone conversation with his dad—the only man he'd ever call *father*. He'd gently filled in the gaps Mark had been too unstrung to hear from his mother. No, they hadn't been *in* love at first, but there'd been something about the petite and pregnant Alicia Navarro that had stirred David Caldwell's protective instincts. He'd had only a year of college left, and since his parents and Alicia's aunt would be helping to support them for the time being, he'd willingly agreed to the marriage.

Then compassion had grown into friendship, which blossomed into genuine love, and once Mark entered their lives, David had realized he was in this marriage for keeps.

"We'd always intended to tell you about your mother and Owen," Dad said. "But with every year that passed, it got harder to find the right time. Besides, with relations already strained between your mother and grandfather, she didn't want the truth driving a wedge between you and your cousins."

Now that Mark had cooled down, he could almost understand their logic, even forgive the secrecy, though it didn't make his next decisions any easier. "This is what Mom meant, isn't it? About me being the one to finally put the past to rest."

"When the reason behind the Navarro-McClement feud came out at your grandfather's birthday party, it was a huge start, but his senility kept him from fully resolving old issues. Now that he's gone…"

Mark pinched the bridge of his nose. "It's up to the heir who's both Navarro and McClement to finish healing the rift."

"Exactly." His father paused. "Think you're up for it, son?"

"Guess we'll find out."

With a lot to process, he kept to himself the rest of the weekend—even tried a few clumsy prayers. He couldn't be sure God was listening, but by Sunday evening, a semblance of peace began to fill him. It was time to break the news to his family.

His family on *both* sides of that ugly barbed-wire fence.

As he sat down to supper with Uncle Hank and Aunt Lois, he mentioned he had some news to share and would they mind if he asked everyone over later. They exchanged curious looks but didn't press for details. With their consent, he texted Samuel and Spencer. Need to talk to everyone about some family stuff. Can you and your wives come to the house around 7:30 tonight? Spencer, please bring Audra, too. It's important.

He could only imagine the speculation floating around. While he wished he could ask Holly to come for moral support, since she wasn't family, explaining her presence would be awkward. Later, after the dust settled, it'd be a comfort to know she was only a phone call away.

And since when had he grown so dependent on her friendship? How long had they known each other now—three weeks? It felt like hardly any time at all, and yet…a lifetime.

Simmer down, Caldwell. Are you sure it's Holly who has you so captivated, or is it only because her son is a balm to your grieving heart?

Between the discovery about his parentage and these unexpected but increasingly undeniable feelings for Davey's mom, could he be any more conflicted?

Samuel arrived first. "Joella couldn't make it. Sophie was getting crabby, so we had to put her to bed. What's up, cuz? Your text sounded serious."

"I'd rather wait till everyone's here." Mark motioned toward the living room, where his aunt and uncle had already taken seats.

A few minutes later, Spencer arrived with Lindsey and Audra.

With everyone present, Mark remained standing, hands stuffed nervously into his jeans pockets while six pairs of eyes bored through him. Even Shadow seemed to sense the tension. Sitting on his haunches, the dog looked up at Mark and leaned hard into his leg, the message clear: *Hang in there. I've got your back.*

Meeting their curious stares, he marshaled his courage. "There's no easy way to say this," he began. Then, as tactfully as he knew how, he described what he'd learned about his mother and Owen McClement.

Their expressions ran the gamut. Uncle Hank's brows shot up briefly before he nodded, as if the revelation was no surprise. Aunt Lois and Samuel looked dazed but sympathetic. Audra and Spencer immediately turned anxious gazes toward Lindsey, who'd begun shaking violently, one hand covering her mouth. Casting a tense frown toward Mark, Spencer drew his wife into his arms and pressed her head against his chest.

Mark felt like he could throw up. "So that's it," he concluded, forcing down a swallow. "I'm half Navarro, half McClement. If this changes how you feel about me, I understand."

No one said anything for a long minute. Then Audra stood and gave him a hug. "Oh, Mark, are you okay?"

She was concerned for *him*, when he'd just announced he was her brother's illegitimate son? He tipped his head toward Lindsey, who seemed calmer but tearful. "I'm more worried about her."

"Give her time." Audra took both his hands. "As for Owen, if you're thinking of connecting with him… I hate to say this about my own brother, but please don't count on much."

"I already have a dad. I don't need another one." Mark shrugged. "Owen should know, of course, but Mom said since she's kept the secret all these years, he deserves to hear it from her."

"Probably wise." Audra drew him close for another heartfelt embrace, her love and acceptance seeping into him.

Over her shoulder, Spencer caught Mark's eye and offered a brief but meaning-filled smile. Without a word, he guided Lindsey from the room, and shortly the back door clicked shut. Audra followed soon afterward, and then Samuel left to share the news with Joella.

Alone with Uncle Hank and Aunt Lois, Mark looked from one to the other. "Am I still welcome here?"

"Of course you are." Now Lois was hugging him. "So long as you're okay identifying with possibly the two most dysfunctional families in Texas."

When she stepped aside, Uncle Hank moved in, his right hand gripping Mark's and his left thumping Mark's back. "It may take time, but I believe this will work out for the best, for all of us."

He gave a silent nod. Needing space, he picked up his jacket and headed outside with Shadow. Beneath a clear, star-studded sky, he gulped cold December air as a two-word prayer found its way to his lips: *Thank You.* He wasn't sure why or how, but he couldn't shake the sense that God truly had been with him this evening.

The urge to hear Holly's voice became irresistible. He pulled out his phone and called. When she answered, he said simply, "I told them."

Mark heard a soft intake of breath. "How did they take it?"

"Better than I could have expected. Well, except for Lindsey. She was pretty upset." He moved to one of the Adirondack chairs, and Shadow hopped into his lap. The dog's silky fur beneath his fingers was calming.

"I knew it would be hard for her." Holly grew quiet for a moment. "Does this change anything about your intention to stay?"

He sensed her question touched on something deeper than his commitment to seeing the building project through…like maybe her feelings for him?

Don't jump to conclusions. She probably just wanted to make sure he wouldn't be leaving Davey high and dry.

"No, nothing's changed. If anything," he said, staring up at the sky, "the truth coming out gives me even more reason to stick around. Seems there may be a greater purpose for my time at the ranch than fulfilling the terms of a will."

The words poured out of him then—his mother's

teenage pregnancy, how his parents came to be married, the friendship that had deepened into true love.

"I don't know how it'll happen or when," he concluded, "but I feel like that stupid old fence has got to come down, and that somehow it's going to be up to me."

Holly felt honored that Mark trusted her enough to reveal his heart this way. The abrasive alpha male who only three weeks ago had chastised her for not knowing where her son was playing seemed far removed from this open, impassioned and much kinder version of Mark Caldwell.

She liked him. More and more every day.

When he'd run out of words and they said their goodbyes, her pulse raced in a way it hadn't since…

Since Blaine.

"Oh, Holly," she murmured, palm pressed to her chest, "you'd better watch your step."

As if her guilt at the possibility of being interested in someone new wasn't bad enough, she knew all too well what happened whenever she dreamed too far into the future.

At the ranch the next morning, Holly found Joella alone at the worktable. "Lindsey's out with Audra and Spencer working the cattle," Joella said. "She's not in a good place emotionally right now."

"I can only imagine what a shock it must have been." Holly set her tote on an empty chair.

Joella stared. "You know?"

Grimacing, she nodded. "Mark called me last night after the family meeting."

A curious smile curled one side of Joella's mouth. "I didn't realize how close you two were getting."

"He needed an impartial listener, that's all." She set her laptop on the table and opened the cover. "About the band banquet, what do you think—"

"I think you're avoiding the topic." Joella reached across the table and used one finger to close Holly's laptop.

She sat back and crossed her arms. "And *I* think my friendship with Mark—and that's *all* it is—should be the least of everyone's concerns at the moment."

"Of course, you're right." Joella's smile softened into an apology. "I'm glad Mark has you to confide in. If he's half as distraught as Lindsey, he needs a good friend."

"I agree." Holly opened her computer once more. "Now, about the band banquet…"

With the noise of power tools drifting their way from the building site, they handled as much business as they could without Lindsey. Holly had errands to run, so she left shortly before noon. She considered stopping on her way out to see how Mark was doing, but he appeared to be in a lengthy discussion with one of his workers.

Besides, she didn't care to fuel the rumor mill.

Her first stop in town was the church. River Bend Events regularly rented their commercial-grade kitchen for food prep, and she had a few things to check on concerning the band banquet. Hosting large functions would be so much easier once they opened their on-site banquet facility with kitchen.

Next, she went to the drugstore downtown to pick up Davey's prescription refill. After parking, she had to walk past the empty storefront she'd seen the other day—the one that reminded her so much of the tearoom Gran had taken her to. A small sign now appeared in front of the faded newsprint covering the window:

Treat Yourself to Free Books and Free Gifts.

Answer 4 fun questions and get rewarded.

◀ **DETACH AND MAIL CARD TODAY!** ▶

	YES	NO
1. I LOVE reading a good book.	◯	◯
2. I indulge and "treat" myself often.	◯	◯
3. I love getting FREE things.	◯	◯
4. Reading is one of my favorite activities.	◯	◯

TREAT YOURSELF • Pick your 2 Free Books...

Yes! Please send me my Free Books from each series I select and Free Mystery Gifts. I understand that I am under no obligation to buy anything, as explained on the back of this card.

Which do you prefer?

❏ **Love Inspired® Romance Larger-Print** 122/322 IDL GRDP
❏ **Love Inspired® Suspense Larger-Print** 107/307 IDL GRDP
❏ **Try Both** 122/322 & 107/307 IDL GRED

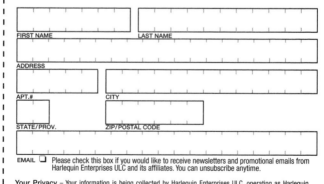

FIRST NAME   LAST NAME

ADDRESS

APT.#   CITY

STATE/PROV.   ZIP/POSTAL CODE

EMAIL ❏ Please check this box if you would like to receive newsletters and promotional emails from Harlequin Enterprises ULC and its affiliates. You can unsubscribe anytime.

LI/SLI-520-TY22

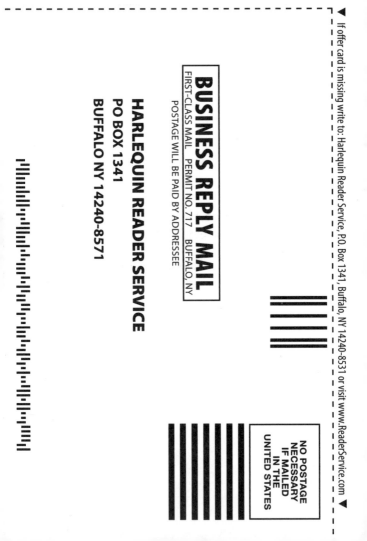

SPACE FOR LEASE
ZONED MIXED-USE
CALL 512-555-2000

Her stomach fluttered. *If only...*

But the timing was all wrong. Besides the whole financing issue, Davey must remain her number-one priority, with her commitment to River Bend Events a close second.

"Thinking about calling?" Mark's voice beside her made her startle.

"Oh, no. Just daydreaming." She composed herself before turning to look at him. "What brought you to town?"

"I need to pick up some stuff from the builders' supply and thought I'd grab lunch at Bonnie's first." He tilted his head. "You wouldn't want to join me, would you?"

"I shouldn't. I—I still have so much to do."

"I understand." His jaw muscles worked. "I wondered if Lindsey said anything this morning."

"Sorry, no, I didn't even see her." At his troubled frown, she touched his arm. "She'll be okay. She just needs—"

"Time. Yeah." His gaze drifted toward the shop window. "She's my half sister, and there's nothing I can do to help either of us come to terms with this."

"I'm sure Audra's talking to her."

"Audra, Aunt Lois, Uncle Hank—even Samuel— they've all expressed their concern and support. So why do I feel more like an outsider than ever?"

Holly searched for something she could say to ease his pain. She came up empty.

"The only thing I know for certain is that I've got to…" His voice faltered. "Got to find a way…"

He stepped forward and reached toward the storefront window. With his index finger, he traced the words of a fading newspaper headline behind the glass: Land Conservancy Preserves a Family's Heritage.

He took his phone from his pocket and snapped a photo of the article, then scanned the rest of the page. "Is this a local paper?"

Holly moved closer, searching for the publication's name. She found it at the top left corner, along with the issue date. "It's an Austin paper, from two months ago. Why is it important?"

"Not sure yet." He photographed the name and date. "Is there a library in town?"

"Yes, a small one. It's around the corner on Hillside." She pointed up the street. "If you want to go there now, I can show you."

Ten minutes later, the librarian set them up at a computer station, where Holly helped Mark access the article online and print out a copy. He briefly studied the page before folding it and slipping it into his inside jacket pocket.

"Are you going to tell me what that's all about?" Holly asked as they left the library.

"It gave me an idea," he said, holding the door for her. "A possible solution to the divided ranches."

"A land conservancy? But how…"

"That's what I have to figure out."

By the time they rounded the corner onto Central Avenue, he was walking almost faster than she could keep up with. When she halted in front of the drugstore, he continued on, but instead of crossing the street to Bonnie's Bistro, he went straight to his truck, parked at the end of the block.

Then, as if suddenly remembering he'd left her be-hind, he paused beside his truck and waved. "Sorry," he called. "We'll talk later."

Wow. Nothing so damaging to a woman's self-esteem as finding herself an afterthought. And to think, only this morning she'd been guilt-ridden over imagining herself attracted to Mark Caldwell.

Driving away, Mark felt bad about deserting Holly on the sidewalk. But with his mind spinning a mile a minute, common courtesy had flown out the window. He wanted to spend more time looking into this land conservancy thing, but he also needed to pick up those supplies and return to the building site so his crews could keep working. Since he'd spent a good portion of his lunch break at the library, a sit-down meal at Bonnie's would have to wait. Instead, he stopped at the Dairy Queen for a burger and fries to go.

What with hopping back and forth between the event center and Samuel's new house during work hours, then spending his evenings doing internet research on the pros and cons of conservancies, the next few days went by in a blur. He'd seen Holly coming and going, but he kept missing the chance to offer even a brief hello.

Did she think he was intentionally avoiding her? How could he blame her, when he'd deserted her after she'd helped him at the library the other day? Kellie'd have a thing or two to say about his manners—or lack thereof.

On Thursday afternoon, as he sat on his open tailgate sipping coffee and reviewing the next phase of construc-tion on the event center, Holly pulled up next to him in her minivan. She lowered the window. "I'm leaving to get Davey from school, but Lindsey asked me to tell you she'd like to talk soon." Chin elevated slightly, she added, "Whenever you can break away."

His stomach plummeted—less because Lindsey was ready to talk and more because of the detachment in Holly's tone. He set down his thermal mug and dropped to the ground. "The week's gotten away from me." He stepped closer. "I apologize for the other day. I should have called."

She gazed out the windshield. "Don't worry about me. But I hope you can make time for Davey again soon."

"How about this afternoon, if you can bring him out my way? Or I'll come into town and we can go to a park or something. Whatever works for you."

Lips pressed together, she released a slow breath through her nostrils. He found himself transfixed by the tiny dimple at the left corner of her mouth.

"I do have a ton of things to catch up on at home," she said, still not looking directly at him. "If it works for you to pick up Davey at the apartment around three thirty and go do something fun for a couple of hours, I know he'd appreciate it."

He did a quick mental rundown of what he'd need to handle at the building sites so he could get away by three. "I'll be there. You can count on me." With a brief smile and nod, she raised her window and continued down the driveway.

A tremor snaked through Mark at the thought that Holly would decide he was too temperamental and emotionally messed up to be around her son. Could he feel any more desperate? Well, yeah, he could. He *had*. Those heartbreaking last moments as his daughter's life slipped away. The defeated, despairing coldness in his wife's eyes as she'd turned her back on him and their marriage. He'd failed Kellie, failed Rae.

He would *not* flake out on Davey.

Getting this attached to the boy had never been part of his plan. Blame Shadow, who'd latched on to Davey from day one, dragging Mark right along with him. Maybe the dog had only been following orders—the "assignment" Kellie had whispered to him with her final breaths: *"Daddy isn't nearly as strong as he wants everyone to believe, so after I go to Heaven, he'll need you to take care of him."*

But why did the overachieving animal have to find him another endearing kid to love? A kid with a pretty, green-eyed mom who, with one hike of her chin, could bulldoze Mark's heart and reduce him to a useless pile of rubble?

This was getting him nowhere. He checked the time—nearly 2:00 p.m. Maybe he should knock off work even earlier and see if he could clear the air with Lindsey before he headed into town. After a quick discussion with Pete Castañeda, the event center foreman, he hopped in the truck and drove down the road to Samuel's homesite. Once he had things lined up with McGee's crew there, he stopped at the ranch house to pick up Shadow, who was more than raring to go.

Then back to the McClement ranch. With Shadow parked at his feet, he sat down with Lindsey in the living room and waited for her to speak first.

She spiraled a dark curl around her index finger. "I'm sorry it's taken me this long to reach out, but I didn't know what to say to a brother I didn't know I had."

He bristled. "If you think it's been any easier for me—"

"I can't even imagine how it would feel to discover

your father isn't really…" Voice trailing off, Lindsey glanced away. "What I've wanted to say is, I don't hold any of this against you. My problem with my—*our*—father is the hurt he caused when he walked out on my mother and me. And all because he never got over losing Alicia."

Mark lowered his head. "My mother told me how in love she'd thought they were. She also said she hadn't understood what real love was until my dad—David—came into her life."

"I can believe it." Lindsey harrumphed. "Owen McClement has never been known for his commitment to family. I found out recently that he and his current wife have separated."

Mark didn't want to imagine what his childhood would have been like if his mother and Owen had stayed together. Judging from the things his mother had told him and how Lindsey described the man…well, Owen McClement didn't sound like much of a man at all.

"Are you going to try to see him?" Lindsey asked.

"Guess it depends on whether he has any interest."

"Trust me—it would only be for whatever he can get out of you." Her mouth firmed. "And if he finds out his son stands to inherit a share of Navarro Quarter Horses, don't say I didn't warn you."

Mark couldn't suppress a wry laugh. "Too bad for him. The verdict on my inheritance is still eleven months away, and it's definitely not a sure thing."

"I hope you won't give up too quickly."

"Unlike what you said about Owen, I try hard to to be a man of my word," he assured her. "But once these buildings are done…wouldn't it be easier all around if I went back to Montana and let Spencer and Samuel divide my share between them?"

"Easier?" Lindsey's jaw dropped. "Why would you think such a thing?"

A dull ache settled in the center of Mark's chest. "For one thing, because I know nothing about ranching. For another…" *I'm getting too close to losing my heart again, and I can't risk it.*

Then he recalled all the notes he'd gathered on land conservancies. He couldn't simply let that idea drop, not when it had the potential to salvage at least a portion of the Navarro-McClement legacy.

If he could only keep his priorities straight. The construction sites. The conservancy. And time with Davey. He'd made a promise, and he'd keep it, no matter what it cost him. In fact, if and when he made the decision to return to Montana, maybe he'd even let Davey keep Shadow. The gift would be a worthy tribute to Kellie… and maybe help him close the door once and for all on that heart-crushing chapter of his life.

Chapter Eight

Several days later, with the high school band banquet behind them and everything falling into place for the Gracey-Totten wedding on Friday, Holly took a morning off to finish her Christmas shopping. It would be another sparse collection of gifts under the tree, but by this time next year, things should be looking up. With the event center on track for completion by mid-April, they were already booking large indoor functions for late spring and early summer, including weddings, graduation parties and family reunions.

Leaving Janeé Clare's with a beaded bracelet for Joella and an infinity scarf for Lindsey, she continued along Central Avenue toward Ally & Aiden Gifts. The shop also carried books for children and teens, and she hoped to find the latest by Davey's favorite author.

As she neared the vacant shop, her steps slowed. The papered-over display window reminded her of the day Mark had noticed the article about land conservancies. Lately he seemed increasingly preoccupied with whatever his research had turned up, but he still made an effort to spend time with Davey. The last couple of Saturdays, the two of them had done more work at the old cabin, and Davey thought it wouldn't be long before Mark had the place habitable. Although why anyone would want to live alone in such rustic and isolated conditions was beyond Holly.

A blurry reflection appeared next to hers in the window glass before a familiar male voice said, "We've gotta stop meeting like this."

She spun around. "Mark. Hi. I was just doing some Christmas shopping."

"Same here." He held up an Ally & Aiden Gifts bag. "I wanted to get a gift for Aunt Lois and Uncle Hank, and Samuel gave me a few suggestions. I found something for Davey, too. Hope he likes joke books."

"He loves them." She was touched that he'd thought to get her son a Christmas present. "G-rated, of course."

"Of course."

Her glance drifted toward the shop window. Out of curiosity, she asked, "Have you learned anything helpful about land conservancies?"

"It's been enlightening. I've scheduled an appointment after the holidays to meet with a representative from Hill Country Farm and Ranch Conservancy."

"I'm not sure I understand how it works."

"Basically, the owners donate a section of land to the conservancy. They can still use the land, but it's now considered a conservation easement, which means it's protected in its natural condition for perpetuity."

Holly recalled the trail ride a few weeks ago and Hank Navarro's concerns about encroachment from the other side of the river. "So...the land would be safe from developers and such?"

"That's the idea. But there are options to consider, so before I present this to my family—on both sides— I need to put together a clear plan."

"I gathered you hadn't told them yet. Don't worry, I haven't mentioned it, either." She shifted the strap of her shoulder bag. "Well, I should finish my shopping."

"Yeah, me, too. When would be a good time to meet with Davey again?"

"He's out of school until after the first of the year, so whenever you can spare a few hours."

"You have a big event this weekend, right?"

"Yes. Friday."

"The work crews are getting a few days off over Christmas, so what if I take Davey for the whole day? He could even spend the night." Hopefulness glistened in his eyes. "He's been asking when we could have a sleepover at the cabin."

She pulled her lips between her teeth. "I'm not sure about overnight. He sleeps with a monitor under his mattress that will trigger an alarm if it senses seizure-like movements."

"Does he have nighttime seizures very often?"

In truth, it had been months. "No, but it's unpredictable. And in an unfamiliar situation…"

Mark gave a thoughtful nod. "Probably not convenient for Davey to bring the monitor along?"

"No, not really." Not to mention the unit was expensive and she wouldn't risk sending it with them to the cabin.

One eye narrowed, Mark scratched his chin. "What if we had a seizure monitor that's entirely portable, extremely reliable and runs on dog food and affection? Would that ease your mind?"

He had her there. Besides, if Davey found out she'd turned down the invitation strictly because he wouldn't have his fancy electronic mattress monitor, he'd hold it against her forever. "I—I'll think about it, okay?"

"Fair enough." He glanced toward the shop window again, his brow furrowing. "The sign's gone."

"Oh, I hadn't noticed." Indeed, the For Lease placard she'd seen there two weeks ago had been removed. A twinge of disappointment stabbed beneath her ribs. Did she really expect the space would still be available if one day in the far, *far* distant future she found the wherewithal to open a tearoom? Unable to hold back a sigh, she said, "Maybe they found a tenant."

Appearing lost in thought, Mark barely acknowledged her remark.

"Okay, then," she said, backing up a step. "We can talk later about arrangements for Friday."

"Right. Friday." With a distracted wave, he turned in the opposite direction and ambled down the sidewalk.

Honestly, it was a complete waste of emotional energy trying to understand the man. Each time she decided that, yes, perhaps this could evolve into a meaningful friendship—or possibly something more—his mood would shift and this...*enigma* would emerge. How could one man be both intriguing and infuriating at the same time?

Had Blaine been any different? Her late husband, whom she'd loved to distraction, certainly had had his maddening moments. Once he'd set his mind on something, he couldn't easily be dissuaded, often despite the logical arguments Holly came up with. The night of his death had been no exception.

Davey had been six, and after they'd all but given up hope of growing their family, she was pregnant again. One December evening, she'd been feeling especially nauseous and craving raspberry sorbet, but they were under a winter storm watch.

"The roads aren't icy yet," Blaine had insisted with

his usual bravado. "I'll run to the supermarket and be back in no time."

Davey was already getting his jacket. "I wanna go, too, Dad. We might see some Christmas lights on the way."

Twenty minutes after they'd left, the weather service broke in on a TV program with a dire update on the winter storm sweeping across the Dallas/Fort Worth area. Why hadn't Blaine listened when she'd argued it wasn't safe, much less taken their son along?

Then the doorbell rang. Two policemen, their dark caps and jackets dusted with white crystals, stood on her porch. "Are you Mrs. Blaine Elliot…?"

Not only had she lost her husband that night, but two days later, she awoke in the hospital to realize she'd lost their baby, too.

Now, glimpsing her reflection in the storefront glass, she brushed away the tear sliding down her cheek. Hadn't she learned her lesson—several times over? *This is the day which the Lord hath made.* This day— today—was all anyone could count on.

So she would not waste her time imagining uncertain if not highly improbable futures—neither tearooms nor interesting new friendships.

And especially not second chances for love.

Sitting in his truck at the end of the block, Mark held his breath as he scrolled through the photos on his phone. When he found the shot of the conservancy article in the shop window, he used two fingers to enlarge the image, then shifted it until the lower right corner came into view.

Yes! He'd managed to capture enough of the leasing information sign to read the phone number.

Seconds later, a woman answered his call. "Shady Grove Property Management. This is Barbara."

"I'm calling about the retail space for lease at 206 Central Avenue in Gabriel Bend. Have you already found a tenant?"

Computer keys clicked. "No, it hasn't been leased. However, the owner has taken the building off the market temporarily while he makes some cosmetic improvements."

Mark barely restrained his relieved exhalation. He hadn't been able to shake the vision of a smiling Holly standing in that doorway as she greeted her tearoom patrons. He'd also ridiculously imagined handing her the signed lease as a Christmas present.

"Sir?" Barbara interrupted his thoughts. "Are you inquiring about leasing the building?"

"Not personally. I was asking for a friend." Thoughts whirling, he drummed his fingers on the steering wheel. "What if I wanted to put a hold on it somehow, until she determines if she can arrange financing for her business venture?"

The woman's soft chuckle indicated he was asking the impossible, which he'd already surmised. Using an exaggerated Texan drawl, she said, "I think you're putting the cart before the horse."

"Would you at least take my phone number? If anyone else should express interest, I'd appreciate a heads-up." Even if it meant digging into his own savings to secure the building for Holly.

"I can do that. You're the first inquiry we've received for this location, so you'll be at the top of the list."

"Thanks, I appreciate it." He gave her his name and number. Then another thought occurred. It'd be wise to determine whether the space could actually work as a tearoom. "Any chance I could make an appointment to see inside?"

"My office is in Georgetown, but let me check my schedule… How about Friday, say, around ten thirty?"

Mark winced. He'd probably have Davey with him by then. But the boy wouldn't have to know exactly why Mark was looking at the building. "Sure, pencil me in."

Deciding he'd been away from the job sites long enough, he headed back. The biggest concern any time of year was weather delays, but with roofing now in place on both Samuel's house and the event center, his foremen agreed things were in order for the planned break over Christmas.

At noon on Thursday, Mark had his crews secure the sites, then sent them home to enjoy a few days off with their families. He figured the River Bend Events ladies would appreciate a progress report on their building, plus he hadn't yet confirmed with Holly what time he should expect Davey tomorrow, so he rapped on the back door of the McClement house.

Audra showed him to the dining room, where Holly, Lindsey and Joella were busy attaching white bows to silver candleholders.

Joella, closest to the door, greeted him with a laugh. "Enter at your own risk."

He lifted both hands. "Just don't put me to work." The women barely paused while he gave them a brief status update on the construction. "So it'll be quiet around here until the middle of next week."

"That'll be a relief." Palm to her forehead, Lindsey gave a dramatic sigh. "I think all the racket has even given the horses and cattle headaches."

"Now that the framing and roofing's done, the worst

should be over." Edging toward the entryway, he asked if he could borrow Holly for a moment.

She excused herself and joined him near the front door. "Are we still on for tomorrow?"

"Absolutely. I wanted to check with you about timing."

"I need to meet my kitchen crew at the church by nine a.m., so I won't be coming out this way. Would you mind picking up Davey in town? If that's too early for you to come by my place, I can bring him to the church to wait."

"No problem—I'm a chronic early riser. What if I swing by around eight thirty?"

"That'd be great!" She rolled her eyes. "Hanging out while I'm busy cooking isn't as fun for Davey as it used to be."

He offered a hopeful smile. "And are we good for an overnight at the cabin?"

"It's all Davey's talked about since I mentioned your invitation. His sleeping bag and backpack are already parked by the door." Her expression grew serious. "Are you sure Shadow would alert you if Davey did have a seizure?"

"He wasn't trained as a seizure alert dog, but if how he reacted that first day I met Davey is any indication, I believe he's a natural. Anyway, I'll be right there, too, and it won't take much to wake me up." He glanced away, his voice softening. "I've been a light sleeper ever since Kellie…"

Holly rested her hand on his forearm. "I'm so sorry, Mark. And I do trust that Davey will be safe with you. It's just… I've lost so much, too, and it's hard to let go."

That much he knew. Which was why he had no business getting this close to Davey—much less to his beautiful mom.

He freed his arm on the pretense of letting himself out the front door. "Tomorrow, then."

"Tomorrow."

You need to dial it back, Caldwell, he told himself on his way out to the truck. *Way, way back.*

On Friday morning, Shadow must have sensed Mark was headed into town for Davey, because the dog hopped into the truck before he could stop him. Tail wagging, Shadow shifted his gaze from the windshield to Mark and back again, as if urging him to put the truck in gear and the pedal to the metal.

"I get it, fella," he said, heading for the road. "We're both getting too attached."

He should have canceled the meeting with the property manager. He had zero business inserting himself into Holly's affairs this way. But did he pick up the phone and make the call? Nope. He convinced himself he was curious to see the building purely from a contractor's perspective. And maybe he'd leave one of his new business cards with the property manager in case the next tenant wanted some remodeling done.

There was no point in driving all the way out to the ranch when he'd only have to turn around and head back to town to make the ten thirty appointment. Instead, he took Davey to Bonnie's Bistro for a hobbit-esque "second breakfast" of blueberry waffles and sausage. The December weather was nice enough that Mark had no concerns leaving Shadow in the truck. He'd parked where he could see the truck from the window—and where Shadow could also see them.

They took their time over breakfast, then Mark

clipped on the dog's leash and they explored downtown for an hour. At twenty past ten, they found a wrought-iron bench two doors down from the vacant shop.

Davey invited Shadow onto the bench between them. "Why are we hanging out here?"

"I'm checking out a retail space."

"What for? Do you need an office for your company?"

"No, not really." But that might be something to consider. *If* he survived his year at the ranch and decided to stay.

"Then why?"

"Just…because." Yep, keeping the appointment was so *not* a good idea.

A silver Mercedes pulled into a parking spot nearby, and a fiftyish woman in a gray pantsuit got out. When she strode toward the empty building with a wad of keys in hand, Mark figured she was the property manager he'd spoken with. He nudged Davey and Shadow off the bench and they headed over.

"Barbara? I'm Mark Caldwell."

"Yes, hello." She extended her hand, then smiled down at Davey. "And this must be your handsome son."

"Ah, no, just a friend." Mark cleared his throat. "Hope it's okay if the dog tags along."

Barbara looked at him askance. "I don't normally…"

"Shadow's my service dog," Davey piped up. "We forgot his vest today, but I have a seizure disorder, and he lets me know if one's coming on."

"Oh!" The woman cast an uneasy glance at Mark. When he shrugged and nodded, she turned to unlock the shop door. "All right, then. Feel free to look around."

On their way inside, Mark discreetly passed the leash to Davey. He perused the open area up front and estimated eight or ten tables could easily fit, with enough room along the side wall for a counter or possibly a display case for Holly's fancy desserts. The hammered-tin ceiling was a nice touch.

Moving closer to Barbara, Mark stepped around a tarp and can of paint. "How's the building plumbed?"

"There are two restrooms down the hall." She pointed behind them. "Also a full commercial sink in the back room."

"Could it be remodeled as a restaurant kitchen?"

"Absolutely. Was your friend thinking of opening a food service establishment?"

"A ladies' tearoom, actually. It's a dream of hers."

Davey tugged on Mark's jacket sleeve. "Are you talking about Mom?"

His stomach sank. He hadn't seen the boy come up beside him. "I was just asking some questions."

"She has an album with old pictures of her and my grandma when they were a *lot* younger. Sometimes they were with my great-grandma, eating in a fancy place with flower vases and lacy stuff and pretty dishes. My great-grandma died a long time before I was born. Mom always looks kind of happy-sad whenever she looks at those pictures."

"Special memories, I'm sure." Barbara tilted her head and smiled, then gestured wide with her arms. "Yes, this could be remodeled into a charming tearoom. Your friend should seriously consider it."

Mark turned away from Davey and spoke through gritted teeth. "I think I mentioned the financial issue?"

The woman's gaze became sympathetic. "No harm in drawing up a business plan and visiting with a bank officer to see what could be worked out."

No harm except getting Holly's hopes up only to risk

disappointment. "We'll see." He took out his phone. "Mind if I snap a few photos?"

Twenty minutes later, he was back in the truck with Davey and Shadow. "Not a word to your mom about our little visit this morning, okay? I'll talk to her about it if and when I decide the time is right."

Davey made a zipping motion across his lips. "Our little secret."

Davey must have had an exceptionally good time at the cabin, because after Mark brought him over to the McClement ranch the next morning, the boy couldn't stop smiling.

Holly and her friends had met to finish putting things in order after the Gracey-Totten wedding and reception. She was too worn out to do much more than listen and nod as Davey regaled her with tales of fishing in the river and cooking their catch over a campfire, then spreading blankets on the ground and stretching out beneath the stars while Mark pointed out the constellations.

"It was cold but *so* fun," her son said as he and Holly toted plastic crates of supplies and decorations out to the storage building. "Afterward, we went inside and Mark lit a fire in the potbelly stove."

"Oh, that's good."

"Yeah, it warmed up fast. He's gonna see about getting electricity soon. Water, too. You've gotta come out sometime and see what all he's done."

"Maybe one of these days." Setting a crate on the shelf, she yawned. Right now, she really needed a nap.

"Mark says they have bigger fish in Montana than here. He likes to go ice fishing in the winter." The kid was still talking a mile a minute. "He said it gets really cold there, and it snows tons, like even in May some-times."

"Brrr! That sounds way too cold for me." Holly started back to the house. She hoped she could keep her eyes open long enough to make it home safely.

"Oh, and it was really cool yesterday when we were in town. We had waffles at Bonnie's Bistro, and then Mark met some lady to see an old building."

Holly's ears perked up. "Which old building?"

"I dunno. It was downtown somewhere. I don't think the lady was gonna let Shadow go in with us until I told her he was my seizure dog. Then she was fine." When Holly stared at him, he looked sheepish. "I wasn't lying, Mom, not really."

She was still stuck on the part about Mark checking out the vacant shop. He'd certainly acted strangely the other day when they'd noticed the sign with the leasing number was missing. "Did Mark say why he wanted to see the building?"

He scrunched his face. "I'm not supposed to tell you."

"Davey!" She took a deep breath to keep from completely losing her cool. In a calmer tone, she said, "Honey, it isn't right for Mark or anyone else to make you promise to keep something from your mother."

"I know, but I think he wanted it to be a surprise." His lower lip stuck out. "Are you mad?"

"No, sweetie, not at you." But she did need to speak to Mark about this. "Wait for me in the house. I'm going next door to find out what this is about."

"But Mom, if he finds out I told you—"

"He had no business asking you to keep secrets from me. Now, go inside. I'll be back soon."

Exhausted as she was, Holly trudged across the field and ducked through the opening in the barbed-wire fence. She'd hoped to find Mark outside so she wouldn't have to disturb the Navarros, but when she didn't see him anywhere, she knocked on the back door.

Lois greeted her with a smile, baby Sophie propped on her hip. "Hi, Holly. Can I help you?"

"I need to talk to Mark." She tried to smile back, but it was a wasted effort.

"You just missed him. He walked out to the cabin to do some more fixing up."

"Oh." Deflating, she looked over her shoulder. Did she have the energy to hike all that way to say what she needed to say?

"Is it important?" Lois asked. "Because I could give you the keys to Mark's truck if you wanted to drive yourself. He won't mind."

"No, it can wait—"

But Lois had already bustled back inside. A moment later, she returned and handed Holly a key fob. "Go ahead, hon. I'd take you myself, but I have a pot of chili on the stove."

By now, she should have learned that no one argued with Lois Navarro. She nodded her thanks, then trekked across the driveway to Mark's dust-coated dark blue Silverado. It took some playing with the seat adjustment levers, but when she could finally see over the steering wheel and reach the gas and brake pedals, she put the truck in gear and steered down the lane toward the cabin.

Five tension-filled minutes later, she parked in the grassy area in front of the cabin. As she shut off the engine, Mark appeared on the stoop, the confusion on his face turning to worry.

He rushed over and yanked open her door. "What are you doing here? Is Davey okay?"

"Davey's fine." She confronted him with a glare. "But you and I need to talk."

Chapter Nine

Mark racked his brain trying to figure out why Holly seemed so upset. He couldn't think of a single thing that had gone even a little bit sideways during his time with Davey, unless…

"Look, Holly, whatever this is about—"

"As if you don't know." She climbed from the truck cab, stumbling as her sneaker caught the running board. He thrust out both arms to grab her, and she fell against his chest. Finding her footing, she pushed free with a huff and shoved her hair out of her eyes.

Why did she have to look so cute just now, righteous indignation and all? He bit the inside of his cheek to resist the sudden urge to laugh. "Are you okay?"

"Yes—no." She glowered at the open truck door, as if the vehicle were somehow to blame for tripping her, then gave the hem of her jacket a sharp tug. "I'm *not* okay because you had no right asking my son to keep secrets. I demand you tell me right this second whatever it was you *didn't* want me to find out about."

Yep, he should have known. Looking down, he toed a rock. "How much did Davey say?"

"Just something vague about meeting a lady at the

vacant building downtown." Head tilted, she planted her fists against her hips. "Why are you so interested in the place? And why take Davey along and then tell him not to tell me?"

Evading her questions would only erode her trust even further. "Want to come inside? I have a nice fire going in the stove."

Her lips twitched to the left. With a shrug, she pushed the truck door shut, then handed him his key fob and grudgingly walked with him to the cabin.

Inside, he gestured toward the pair of scarred spindle-back chairs. The candy cane–striped seat pads Aunt Lois had supplied added a festive touch. Not that he was all that into Christmas, but the dreary cabin could certainly use some brightening up.

Holly stepped around Shadow where he napped on a small braided rug, then sat gingerly and extended her hands toward the warmth of the stove. She glanced around the room. "The place definitely looks better than the last time I saw it."

"Thanks. It's almost livable—or will be, once I connect electricity and dig a well and septic tank." He brought over two mugs from the pie safe. With a nod to the enameled pot on the stove, he said, "Coffee? It's not fresh, but it's hot."

She waved away his offer. "Can we skip past the pleasantries? I need you to answer my question."

This wasn't how he'd pictured his big reveal, but it was probably what he deserved for taking matters into his own hands. He stalled by pouring coffee for himself. "I wanted to do something nice for you," he mumbled without looking at her. "That's all."

"Humph. That isn't much of an explanation." Was there perhaps *slightly* less rancor in her tone?

He sank onto the other chair and blew across the steaming sludge in his cup before taking a sip. "There was something in your expression that day in town—remember, the first time we came across the vacant building? You mentioned wishing you could open a tearoom like the one your grandmother took you to."

"Oh, I was just rambling." Her attempt at a dismissive laugh didn't fool him. Turning serious, she looked over at him. "What does that have to do with this secret of yours?"

"I thought if I determined the building could be remodeled as a restaurant, you could put together a business plan and maybe set the wheels in motion." Saying it out loud *really* made him sound like he was butting his nose in where it didn't belong. "I'm sorry. It's your life, your dream. I should have stayed out of it."

Gazing through the stove grate into the flames, she exhaled softly. "It's been a long time since anyone cared so much about my dreams. Not that Lindsey and Joella wouldn't bend over backward for anything I wanted or needed, but I'm not sure I ever told them about the tearoom." She gulped and glanced away. "Honestly, I don't know why I mentioned it to you."

"Just don't be cross with Davey, okay? I asked him not to say anything because I wanted to tell you myself."

She nodded. "I should have realized you had good intentions. But when my son is involved…" A rueful smile tugged up her lips as she raised both hands and curled her fingers. "My tiger claws come out."

"So I noticed." He set his mug on the floor, then leaned forward, arms braced on his thighs. In for a penny, in for a pound, as Grandma Caldwell used to say. "Would it be okay if I tell you what I learned about the building? That way, you can make an informed decision."

"There's nothing to decide," she said with a snort. "I am in no position right now to even consider such a risky business venture."

"I've had your cooking, remember? *Risky* is not how I'd describe your chances of success." When she still seemed doubtful, he hurried on. "Look, what's to lose by drawing up a business plan and talking to a loan officer? At least go take a look at the inside. When you see the potential there—"

"Stop. I can't let you get my hopes up like this. It would never work." Yet something in those big green eyes said she longed to believe otherwise.

Next thing he knew, he was holding her hand. Could he dig this hole he'd fallen into any deeper? "If I can step out of my comfort zone to spend a year on a horse ranch—which I absolutely did *not* want to do—you can certainly take a leap of faith toward something you've wanted to do practically your whole life."

She bit her lip. "I've never created a business plan, not even when I started my home-based catering business. The details just sort of fell into place."

"It's not as hard as it sounds. Lindsey or Joella could help you, or…" He swallowed. Seemed like his hole was filling up with quicksand, and he was about to drown in it. "Or I could."

Not five minutes after Mark drove her back to the McClement house, Holly was mentally berating herself for imagining she could possibly have her tearoom. *Submit a business plan? Apply for a loan?* Right, a single mom with only a dream and a talent for cooking—and no other assets to speak of? The whole idea was pre-posterous.

She buried such yearnings in the farthest corner of her heart and focused on what mattered most—making this a happy Christmas for her son. She'd have loved to take Davey to visit her parents in Albuquerque, where they'd retired several years ago, but airfare wasn't in the budget right now, and Dad's heart condition kept him and Mom from traveling to Texas. Blaine's parents, who lived in the Dallas area, usually spent the holidays with Blaine's sister and family in South Carolina. Though the Elliots doted on Davey, Holly was pretty sure they privately held her at fault for the deaths of their son and unborn grandchild. She could hardly blame them when she still struggled to forgive herself.

The blessing in all this was getting to celebrate Christmas here in Gabriel Bend with her two best friends and their families. Since Audra and Lois enjoyed cooking almost as much as Holly, they had a great time collaborating and preparing a delectable Christmas feast.

With the ebb and flow of togetherness between the Navarro and McClement households, Holly deftly avoided further pressure from Mark about looking into the tearoom possibilities. Then, a few days after Christmas, he had his crews back at work on the event center and Samuel and Joella's house. In addition, River Bend Events had been hired to organize and cater the church's New Year's Eve party, which kept Holly busy that week preparing hors d'oeuvres and desserts to serve three hundred.

Once the holidays had passed and Davey was back in school, life began to settle into a more normal routine. When Holly drove out to the ranch each day to work with Lindsey and Joella, watching the progress on their building made her heart lift. The projected April completion was about as far ahead as she could allow herself to envision. Anything beyond that invited too much uncertainty. Just like the psalm said, she'd give thanks and be glad for today. The future was best left in God's hands.

One morning in mid-January, Mark waved Holly over as she drove past the building site. She pulled to the side of the driveway and parked near his truck. Lowering her window, she couldn't help admiring his stride as he came around the minivan. "What's up?"

"I wanted you to take a look at the kitchen setup one more time while we can still make minor adjustments."

"Okay." As she stepped from the van, he handed her a white helmet similar to his.

Picking her way around construction materials, she followed him inside, where the roar of power tools echoed even louder. Across the large banquet hall, he guided her through a framed opening where eventually double swinging doors would lead to the kitchen.

"Over there's the space where your refrigerator will go," he said, pointing. "And the range and ovens will be between these two counters. Look good so far?"

"Everything's sized for the appliances we have on order, right?"

"Of course." His affronted tone implied, *Don't you trust me?*

So they were back to the prickly Mark Caldwell. She looked down her nose at him, not easy considering their height difference. "It was a simple observation. I wasn't questioning your work."

"Sorry, I'm a little on edge." He removed his helmet

briefly to run his sleeve across his brow. "I've been pulled in several different directions lately."

"Yeah, I can see that." She hesitated. "Since the holiday break ended, Davey's been asking when you'll have time for him again."

He looked even more chagrined. "Let me finish showing you around. Then we can get out of here and talk where it's quieter."

After a look at the walk-in pantry, storeroom and food prep areas, Holly found nothing she'd change. Mark said something to one of the workers, then escorted her outside. She stopped near her minivan and handed him the helmet. "If you're too busy for Davey right now, just say so. I'll help him understand."

"No, I'll make time soon, I promise. It's just that I'm trying to get this conservancy plan worked out, and then last weekend I flew up to Missoula to see my folks and handle some business details."

"I didn't realize you'd been away." And why should she feel hurt that he hadn't mentioned his trip when they'd hardly done more than nod to each other the last couple of weeks?

"It was kind of a last-minute trip," he admitted. "When I came for my grandfather's funeral, I had no idea I'd be sticking around this long. I'd left things up in the air with my construction company back home."

Back home. So he hadn't yet fully embraced Gabriel Bend or the Navarro ranch as home. Holly couldn't blame him. Though she loved her new life here—for the most part, anyway—she still sometimes thought of Waxahachie as home.

She still missed the life she and Blaine would have shared with Davey and the little sister he should have had.

A dream…that's all it ever was.

"Holly?" Mark lightly touched her arm.

She sniffed and drew her thoughts to the present. "I need to get inside. We're having a Zoom conference with an out-of-town client." Pulling open the van door, she pasted on a smile. "I'll explain to Davey that you've been really busy lately. Text me whenever you can spare some time for him."

"I will. Maybe this weekend?"

"Sure." But would he? Doubt and disappointment gnawed at her as she climbed behind the wheel. With a brief wave, she continued up the drive to the parking area.

In the house a few minutes later, she peeled off her jacket and deposited her things at the worktable. Lindsey was setting up her computer for the online meeting while Joella completed a phone call.

"Did I see you talking to Mark out there?" Lindsey asked.

"He wanted me to take a look at the kitchen space." Pulling a chair around, she hastily changed the subject. "Are we about ready to log on?"

"Not quite. Our client's running a little late. In the meantime, we should—"

Holly's phone rang. She swiveled to grab her purse. When she read the school's name on the display, her stomach flipped. Why would they be calling unless something had happened with Davey? She answered warily.

"Hello, Mrs. Elliot. This is Mrs. Hinkhouse from Davey's school." The principal—this couldn't be good. "I'm sorry to tell you that Davey has been in a fight. I have him and the other boy in my office. How soon can you be here?"

* * *

Mark was about to drive over to check on progress at Samuel's house when he glimpsed Holly marching across the backyard—and she was clearly upset. Concerned, he loped across the driveway, intercepting her in front of the chapel.

He halted her with an extended hand. "Holly, slow down. What's wrong?"

"It's—it's Davey." Looking past him, she gave her head a distracted shake. "I have to get to the school."

Panic rose in Mark's chest. "Did he have another seizure?"

"No. He got in a fight."

"A *fight*?" This didn't sound anything like the kid Mark had come to know. "Over what?"

"I don't know yet. I'm on my way to the principal's office to find out." She tried to step around him.

"Wait. Are you sure you're calm enough to drive? Let me take you in my truck."

"No, you're busy. I'll be fine."

"I'm not too busy—" As if to mock his good intentions, his cell phone interrupted with a strident ring. Grimacing, he pulled it from his jeans pocket. Great. The conservancy rep would have to call at this exact moment. Signaling Holly to wait, he answered.

"Mr. Caldwell, it's Ben Bryan. Just confirming our plans for this afternoon."

"Yes, two thirty, right? Can you hold on a sec?" Mark held the phone to his chest and faced Holly.

Before he could push words from his mouth, she met his gaze for the first time since he'd approached. "Really, Mark, I'm perfectly capable of taking care of this situation. There's no need for you to concern yourself." A tight smile flattened her lips. "Don't keep your caller waiting."

Mark watched helplessly as she strode to her minivan and roared down the driveway.

He lost track of how much time had passed before he remembered Mr. Bryan. His hand shook slightly as he returned the phone to his ear. "Sorry, I was in the middle of something."

"No problem. We can talk more when I see you. I'm looking forward to the tour of your property." The man said goodbye and clicked off.

Between worrying about Holly and Davey and getting his thoughts in order to meet with Ben Bryan, Mark wasn't sure how he'd make it through the rest of the morning. He suspected Holly would be too consumed with her son's issues to return after meeting with the principal. And considering how they'd parted ways, he didn't feel good about calling to ask how things went. Holly was irritated with him and had every right to be after the way he'd let her and Davey down these past couple of weeks.

He had to put his guilt on hold, though, until after he met with the conservancy rep. On Monday evening, he'd had a long discussion with Uncle Hank about his initial conversations with Mr. Bryan, and Mark was encouraged by how receptive his uncle had been. He had yet to speak with Audra and Lindsey, but he'd better do so before venturing into McClement backcountry with a stranger.

After covering a few things with the site foreman at Samuel's new home, he gave Lindsey a call to ask if she and her aunt had time to talk.

"Is this about the conservancy?" Lindsey's tone rang with enthusiasm. "Spencer and Samuel heard all about it from their dad last night. Audra loves the idea, and we're excited to learn more."

He told her about his upcoming appointment. "After Mr. Bryan sees the land, he can tell us whether this is even feasible. But after all the years of the feud, I'm hoping this could be a way to unite our families in a common purpose."

"Could Audra and I come along this afternoon?"

"That'd be great. Mr. Bryan is trailering his own horse to the ranch, and we're planning to ride out with Uncle Hank around two thirty."

"We'll be saddled up and ready."

The norther blowing in that afternoon made for a cold and blustery ride. Shadow had wanted to come along, but Mark felt it best to leave him at the house with Aunt Lois so he wouldn't become a distraction. Thankfully, with Hank and Audra assisting Mark with host duties, the tour seemed to be going well.

"This is natural beauty well worth preserving," Ben Bryan said, obviously impressed. Near the fence line between the Navarro and McClement ranches, he reined his bay toward an expansive view of the river and the hills beyond. "You say the strip of land on the other side of the river is also your property?"

Hank rode up beside Mr. Bryan. "See the fence just this side of the ridge? That's where our ranch ends."

"Same for the McClement property," Audra said, one hand holding her hat firmly in place against the wind. "Our fathers made sure this section of river was entirely on our land."

The conservancy rep nodded his approval as he snapped several more photos. "I've seen enough to finalize my report for the board. Let's head back before this weather gets any worse."

Fine with Mark. The wind was making his horse skittish, and if things got dicey, he had zero confidence in his ability to keep his seat. Good thing he'd chosen to wear a riding helmet over looking macho in the Stetson Spencer and Samuel had given him for Christmas.

His ears felt frostbitten by the time they made it safely back to the barn, but beneath his flannel shirt and down jacket, he dripped nervous sweat. He gladly handed the antsy gelding off to one of the stable hands. For the millionth time, he questioned the wisdom of committing to a year at the Navarro ranch. If this conservancy plan worked, though, he could renounce his inheritance in good conscience and return to Montana satisfied he'd done at least one good thing for the Navarro and McClement families.

Aren't you forgetting something? Holly and Davey are here, not in Montana.

Like it mattered. Staying on the woman's good side seemed beyond his abilities. He only hoped the conservancy arrangement fared better than his attempts to move things along for her tearoom.

"…and the review process takes time," Ben Bryan was saying, "but I'm pretty confident the board will decide in your favor."

Mark gave himself a mental shake. "Okay, then. We'll wait to hear from you. Anything we should be doing in the meantime?"

"Both families should engage the services of an attorney and financial adviser. I can refer you to professionals we've done business with in the past."

"We'd appreciate it. Thanks." Mark shook the man's

hand, then got out of the way while he loaded his horse into the trailer.

As Mr. Bryan drove away, Lindsey cast Mark an approving smile. "This is an amazing idea. How'd you ever come up with it?"

His mind flew back to the day he'd stood in front of the vacant shop window with Holly. He swallowed hard before replying. "I saw a newspaper article about conservancies. It sounded intriguing."

Uncle Hank cast his gaze across the ranch. "I wish we'd known about conservancies before your grandfather died. I believe he'd have enjoyed seeing a portion of his land preserved for posterity."

"I know my parents would have been honored," Audra said. A tear in her eye, she clapped Mark on the shoulder. "I'm so proud of you, *nephew*."

At her emphasis on the last word, Mark ducked his head. "I'll get back to you as soon as I hear from Mr. Bryan with those references."

Audra nodded and mounted up to ride next door. Uncle Hank gave Mark a pat on the back before leading his horse to the barn.

Lindsey lingered, a concerned look shadowing her gaze. "I realize we're still getting used to being brother and sister, but I hope you know you can talk to me about…anything."

He narrowed one eye. "Anything. Meaning…?"

"Meaning, when are you and Holly going to quit dancing around what's obviously happening between you?"

His attempt at a dismissive laugh came out more like a snort. "There's nothing between us. We're just friends." And barely so, at the rate things were going.

"That's not the vibe I've been getting, and my romance radar's been pretty accurate lately." Lindsey snickered. "Just ask Samuel and Joella."

Mark had no words—at least none he felt ready to share with his annoyingly perceptive half sister.

A gust of wind rattled the barn door behind them and made Lindsey's horse prance. "Easy, Flash," she soothed with a pat to the sorrel's neck.

Sorrel. Glad to shift mental gears, Mark congratulated himself for remembering the correct term for the horse's reddish-brown color. Still, that didn't mean his uncle and cousins would ever turn him into a horseman. He had Kellie to thank for the countless hours he'd spent at the library checking out horse books for her and then reading along as she pored over the pictures and memorized the stories. If only she'd gotten her transplant. If only she could have had her own horse like she'd always dreamed.

So much for moving on to more upbeat topics.

He should have found a place for Kellie to go riding before she'd gotten so impossibly weak. But no, all he'd wanted was to protect her, bubble wrap her, keep her safe and alive for as long as humanly possible. Because obviously God wasn't doing His part.

Sorry, Lord. I know I've been trying harder to trust You lately. If only You hadn't stayed silent and distant while my baby girl got sicker and sicker. If only You could have healed her...

Realizing Lindsey was staring at him, brows drown together in concern, he drew a gloved hand across his face. "Brrr, we should get in out of this wind. It's making my eyes water."

Her frown said she wasn't buying his explanation for the dampness on his cheeks. "Uh-huh. Well, keep us posted about the conservancy stuff. And I mean it," she added sternly. "You can talk to me anytime."

All he could do was nod.

Chapter Ten

*F*ighting? What had her son been thinking? After the meeting in the principal's office yesterday, it was all Holly could do to keep her eyes on the road as she'd driven Davey home from school. His two-day suspension seemed merciful, considering the bloody nose he'd given his opponent. Davey had come away with little more than bruised knuckles, a few scratches and a torn shirt.

"I'm sorry, Mom." Davey had repeatedly apologized through angry tears. "He just made me so mad."

Apparently, a classmate had called him a baby because of his epilepsy, and Davey had overreacted. Holly had nearly bitten through her tongue to keep from spouting off a few choice names she'd like to call the other boy's mother, who'd seemed a bit too cavalier about the whole thing.

"Boys will be boys," the woman had said with a condescending smirk. *"Your son needs to toughen up and get over himself."*

After breakfast, Holly sat her son down at the kitchen table and told him to get started on the schoolwork his teacher had sent home with him.

Davey locked his arms across his chest and stared out the window. "I'm never going back to school. *Ever.*"

"Not an option, son. And before this day ends, I expect you to compose a written apology, which you will then deliver in person."

"What? No way!"

"Yes, *way.* Other people's rudeness doesn't justify your own bad behavior."

While he grumbled and opened his math book, she put the teakettle on to boil. After a night of tossing and turning, she'd need several cups of stout Irish breakfast tea to clear her head.

A few minutes later, she carried her phone and a steaming mug to the sitting area. Situated in her favorite chair, she called Joella. "I'm going to stay home with Davey this morning," she told her friend. "Text or call if anything comes up that you need me to handle."

Joella offered a sympathetic sigh. "How is our juvenile delinquent this morning?"

"Not a happy camper." She lowered her voice. "On top of everything else, I found out he's struggling in three subjects. Mrs. Nolte says he's gotten lazy about completing assignments."

"I thought spending time with Mark was helping his attitude."

"Hold on a sec." Holly slipped into her bedroom and eased the door closed. "Sorry, I didn't want Davey overhearing. I'm kind of annoyed with Mark right now. He hasn't made time for Davey since the Christmas holidays."

"I know he's been busy at the construction sites, plus now he's working on a shared land conservancy plan for the ranches."

"Oh, you've heard?"

"Yes, a couple of days ago." Joella paused. "You knew about it already?"

"He asked me not to say anything." She winced. "I shouldn't have agreed. Keeping secrets isn't right."

"No harm done. He probably wanted to get all the facts first."

"Still, people shouldn't go meddling in other people's lives."

A thoughtful silence preceded Joella's next words. "That sounds mighty personal. Care to elaborate?"

"Just something I'd mentioned in passing and Mark decided to take matters into his own hands."

"Okay, now you *really* have to explain."

Holly pressed her eyes shut. Joella would never let this drop until she told her. Pulling in a deep breath, she said, "You know the vacant building on Central, down the block from Ally & Aiden's?"

"Yes, I've noticed it."

"I ran into Mark there a couple of months ago and foolishly let slip a childhood dream of someday having my own tearoom. A few weeks later, Mark inquired about the building on my behalf." She harrumphed. "Now he thinks I should create a business plan and apply for a start-up loan."

"That's a great idea! Have you started working on it yet?"

Holly nearly choked. "Well, no. The whole thing's preposterous."

"Lindsey, get in here," Joella called away from the phone. "I'm putting you on speaker, Holly. Hold on." She repeated everything Holly had just told her.

Lindsey gasped. "Stay right where you are, young lady. Jo-Jo and I are on our way over."

She stared at her silent phone. Wonderful. Now what had she done?

Stomach lurching, she went to check on Davey, relieved to find him toiling away on a math problem. He paused only long enough to shoot a poison-dart glare in her direction.

Holly hated being at odds with her son but knew she couldn't cave on this matter. She spied her forgotten tea on the side table and popped the mug in the microwave. Taking her reheated drink to the window, she awaited her friends' arrival while mentally itemizing all the reasons why her frivolous flight of fancy could never become a reality.

But once Lindsey and Joella had her trapped between them on the sofa, they dodged her every attempt to argue. Laptop propped on her knees, Lindsey hammered out an outline for a business plan while Joella chimed in with suggestions. Holly was left with no choice but to set her brain on automatic and supply relevant details.

At one point, Davey came over and knelt on the other side of the coffee table. "And you should call it the For-get-Me-Not Café."

Something twisted in Holly's heart. "Davey," she said softly, "what made you think of that name?"

"Whenever you showed me those pictures with your grandma from when you were little, you always said forget-me-nots were her favorite flowers."

Lindsey squeezed Holly's hand. "It's a perfect name for your tearoom." A moment later, she'd added it to the business plan. "There. Except for refining the income and expense estimates, that's the icing on the cake." She chortled. "Icing. Cake. I made a tearoom pun!"

Groaning, Joella looked toward the ceiling. "Better

stick with finances, Linds. Leave the jokes to the professional comedians."

Holly barely heard her friends' bantering. Head spinning, she couldn't decide whether to thank them for their expertise or to run screaming from the apartment.

In the meantime, Davey had pulled out the old photo album. Joella moved to the other side of Lindsey while the boy pointed out pictures from Holly's birthday lunches with her mother and grandmother.

Davey left them exclaiming over the photos and scooted onto the sofa beside Holly. "You should really do this, Mom. It's what you've always wanted, isn't it?"

"Maybe…once. But it'd be a huge investment of time, not to mention money we don't have."

"Mark said you could get a bank loan. And he'd help you fix up the building to make it just like the one your grandma took you to."

No, no, no! her mind shouted. *Don't you dare let yourself dream again.*

But it was too late. Mark had opened the door on the possibilities. Her two best friends had just helped her draft a business plan. And now, with her son adding his encouragement, she could feel hope and enthusiasm surging.

Yes, she might end up disappointed. But what if she didn't? What if all this unexpected support for her dream was God's nudge toward an even better life for her and Davey?

Didn't she owe it to her son and herself to find out?

Mark hadn't seen Holly since she'd rushed off to the school Wednesday morning. He'd heard about Davey's suspension—poor kid. Poor Holly, too, stuck at home with her son for two days straight. She must be ready for a break. He should offer to bring Davey out to the cabin this weekend. Besides, they were long overdue for an outing.

After lunching on a sandwich and bag of chips while sitting in his truck, he gave Holly a call.

"Hello, Mark." Her greeting sounded a little stressed. No surprise.

"Hi. I've been thinking about you." He cleared his throat. "You and Davey, I mean. How's it going?"

"Not one of our better weeks." Speaking away from the phone, she said, "Davey, I told you to finish cleaning your room."

"But is that Mark?" the boy said in the background. "I haven't seen him and Shadow in forever."

"Actually," Mark interrupted, "that's why I'm calling. I was hoping maybe tomorrow—"

"I don't think so," Holly replied. "Davey's privileges are restricted until he returns to school on Monday."

"Mo-om!"

"Your room, Davey. Now."

Yikes. Things at the Elliot household were worse than Mark had imagined. "I've caught you at a bad time."

"No, wait." A sigh whispered across the connection. "Sorry for sounding snappish, but being cooped up with a grouchy ten-year-old is wearing on me."

"Then it seems like you could both stand a change of scenery."

"You're not wrong." Holly hesitated. "In fact, there is something I'd like to talk to you about."

Mark considered his afternoon agenda—nothing his foremen couldn't handle. "If you need to get out, I could meet you somewhere."

"I can't. It'll take my son the rest of the day to

straighten up his room, and I don't want to give him the idea I'm going soft."

"Then I'll come to your place. Give me an hour to put a lid on things here and I'll be on my way."

"Thank you, but…it'd be better if you didn't bring Shadow."

"I get it. No worries."

When Holly opened the door to him shortly after two, Davey trotted up beside her with a hopeful smile. When he realized Shadow hadn't come along, he let out a disappointed groan.

"Maybe next time," Mark murmured, tousling the boy's blond hair. To Holly, he said, "After the cold front the other day, it's turned into a sunny and mild afternoon. Want to talk outside on the stairs?"

She nodded, then slipped on a sweater. Instructing Davey to get back to his cleaning, she grabbed her laptop off the kitchen table.

A few seconds later, they sat hip to hip on the first step down from the landing. Mark couldn't recall being quite this close to Holly before, and he liked it. A lot. An enticing scent of vanilla and cinnamon emanated from her hair. He wondered if she'd been baking.

When she opened her computer, he said, "This looks serious."

"It kind of is." Tapping some keys, she raised an eyebrow in his direction. "And it's all thanks to you."

His pulse kicked into a higher gear. What had he done this time? Except…she looked more excited than angry. Maybe he should keep his mouth shut and let her explain.

"Actually, thanks to you and my blabbermouth son," she amended. "Lindsey and Joella found out about my long-held hope of opening a tearoom, so they ambushed me the other day and insisted on helping me draft a business plan." She slid her laptop onto his thighs. "This is what they came up with, along with a few ideas of my own."

He swallowed a laugh that was both relief and surprise. "You really did it."

"I haven't done anything yet." Gazing across the backyard, she hugged herself. "I'm still not sure I can follow through."

Mark used the track pad to page through the document. With the exception of a couple of sections that needed more detail, her friends had done an excellent job of incorporating the relevant information. "This is good. Really good. I can help you fill in the blanks."

"I was hoping so. When it comes to remodeling costs, fixtures and such, I'm at a loss."

The fact that Holly trusted him enough to ask his advice made his chest warm. He pulled out his phone. "Can you air-drop the file to me? I'd like to work on it over the weekend."

She reclaimed her computer and hit several keys. "There, you should have it."

He checked his screen to verify. "Thanks for letting me help." He pushed up from the step, then offered his hand as she rose. "Am I forgiven for sticking my nose in where it wasn't wanted?"

Chuckling, she rolled her eyes. "I'll let you know after I see how far this goes."

"Then I have nothing to worry about." He reluctantly released her hand and started down the stairs. He paused to look up at her. "Are you sure I can't get Davey out of your hair for a few hours this weekend? It might be good for both of you."

"You could be right. How about Sunday?" She put

a finger to her chin. "You could join us for church and Sunday dinner, then take Davey to the ranch afterward."

His stomach tensed. Easing back into prayer was one thing, but church? "I don't know…"

"Late service is very casual and friendly. Please?"

When she looked at him that way—he couldn't deny her. He choked down the boulder in his throat. "What time?"

"It starts at ten thirty. But you should get there fifteen minutes early so we can claim a good seat. Davey and I will watch for you out front."

A good seat for Mark would be out in the parking lot. Not trusting his voice, he gave a brisk nod and a wave, then marched down to his truck.

After Kellie died, not even his parents had been able to talk him into returning to church. That a woman he'd known barely two months could entice him to change his mind said a lot.

She should have known he'd be a no-show.

Holly and Davey waited for Mark outside the church doors until 10:35. Giving up, they slipped inside during a praise song and squeezed into seats in the back row. For the next hour, Holly did her best to maintain a worshipful frame of mind. If she succumbed to blame and aggravation, she'd only make Davey's disappointment worse.

Arms locked across his chest, her son stared out the side window as they drove home. "Mark must not like me anymore."

Holly pretended not to notice the tears he tried to hide. "Of course he still likes you. Something must have come up, that's all." Why she defended the man, she had no idea. "When we get home, I'll call and ask

what happened. I'm sure he wouldn't stand us up without good reason."

Or maybe he would. "I, uh, may be catching something," Mark said, not sounding the least bit sick.
"Didn't want to spread it to you and Davey."

"You could have at least texted." Holly lifted the slow
cooker lid to check the savory chicken and dumplings
recipe she'd started earlier that morning. Too bad Mark
would be missing out on the feast.

"I put it off too long and then was afraid of disturb-
ing you during church."

"My phone was on vibrate. It wouldn't have been a
problem." She smiled at Davey, who was watching her
from across the room, and made an effort to lighten
her tone. "Well, take care of yourself and feel better
soon. 'Bye!"

Without giving him a chance to respond, she ended
the call.

"He's sick?" Davey asked.

"Apparently so. Wasn't it nice of him to be consider-
ate of our health?" She flashed a smile. "Would you set
the table, hon? It'll be just the two of us."

Afterward, as she stored the leftovers, Davey said,
"You should take some to Mark. It might make him
feel better."

"I'm sure Mrs. Navarro is looking after him."

Davey moved between Holly and the refrigerator.
"Come on, Mom. Before we moved here, you always
used to take meals to sick people."

Hard getting around a ten-year-old's logic. And she
couldn't easily refuse without making herself look like
the bad guy. Besides, maybe Mark really was coming
down with something. Lindsey had mentioned how cold

and blustery it had been when they'd taken the conservancy rep for a tour of the ranches.

But that was four days ago, and he'd seemed perfectly fine on Friday.

Cool it, Holly. Why can't you give the man the benefit of the doubt?

"Okay, okay." She did an about-face and set the container of leftovers on the table. "Get your jacket and we'll drive out to the ranch."

Half an hour later, she parked in the Navarros' driveway next to an unfamiliar vehicle with Oklahoma license plates. "Davey, you'd better stay in the van. It looks like they have company, so I'm just going to drop this off and we'll be on our way."

Her son wasn't happy about being excluded but obeyed without argument.

Covered dish in hand, she knocked on the back door. When Mark answered, she stared at him in surprise.

"I saw you drive up," he said, looking sheepish. His gaze fell to the container she carried. "What's this?"

"The chicken and dumplings you would have had for lunch today." She thrust it into his hands. "But you look like you're feeling much better." Keeping the sarcasm out of her voice proved impossible.

His chin fell to his chest. "I blew it this morning, and you have every right to be upset. The truth is, I really was sick to my stomach, but not because of anything contagious. I just…" A ragged sigh tore through him as he stared at the container of leftovers. "I couldn't make myself set foot inside a church building, not with all this anger toward God that I can't seem to let go of."

All Holly's resentment drained away. "Oh, Mark."

"I actually did make it into town," he said with a snort. "Even drove around the block a few times trying to work up the nerve to pull into the parking lot. But when I realized I was literally about to lose my breakfast, I turned around and headed home."

She shouldn't ask, but she couldn't help herself. "Did you get here in time?"

He winced. "That would be a no. Thankfully, there wasn't much traffic where I pulled over."

All she could do was shake her head in sympathy.

"Is Davey really bummed with me?"

"He was, until I told him you were sick. Now he's just concerned." Holly offered an embarrassed smile. "He was the one who insisted I bring you a meal."

"Well, thank him for me, and apologize again."

"He's in the van, if you're up to a short visit."

"This isn't exactly a good time." Glancing over his shoulder, Mark firmed his jaw. "Lindsey's here. With her—*our*—father. He showed up out of the blue about twenty minutes ago."

"Oh, no." Holly retreated a step. "You should have said something sooner."

"I was actually glad for a reason to leave the room." He ran a finger around the neck of his pullover. "To say it's awkward in there would be a gross understatement."

"I can only imagine. Is Audra here, too?"

"No, she thought we should work this out between ourselves. Although what there is to work out, I'm not sure." Shaking his head, he coughed out a harsh laugh. "If only I could have made it to church and Sunday dinner with you, I might have avoided this visit entirely."

"But you'd still need to face him sooner or later. Maybe everything is working out exactly the way God wanted it to."

He looked at her askance. "You really believe that, don't you?"

"I believe God is always at work in our lives." She stepped closer and touched his arm. "I know your faith was shaken when your daughter died. I struggled mightily when Blaine was killed and I lost…" Her throat clenched, and she had to glance away. "I lost our unborn child."

"Holly—"

"Please. Don't." She absolutely would not cry. "What I'm trying to say is that God's okay with our doubts and anger. Nothing we can say, think or do will ever cause Him to stop loving us. So I'm going to pray for Him to comfort your grieving heart and to bring peace between you and Lindsey and your father."

Before he could say anything, she backed away and hurried to the van.

As she climbed in and shut the door, Davey shifted to face her. "Mom, you talked forever. Is Mark better?"

"He is, but he has a visitor." She hadn't yet explained to her son about Mark's parentage. That complicated topic seemed better addressed when he was a few years older. Besides, it should be up to Mark to reveal when he felt ready.

And by then, he might have already moved back to Montana and the explanation wouldn't matter.

She really, *really* needed to fight harder to resist whatever these feelings were for Mark Caldwell. Exasperation one minute, empathy the next, and beneath it all an undeniable attraction and the growing sense she wanted him to stay in Gabriel Bend for a long, long time.

Chapter Eleven

Returning to the living room, Mark halted beside Lind-sey's chair. She sat stiffly on the opposite side of the room from Owen McClement, who'd taken the far end of the sofa. Uncle Hank and Aunt Lois had politely excused themselves.

Owen clasped his hands between his knees. "Like I told Lindsey when I first got here," he began, "I didn't come to cause trouble." His gaze shifted between them, then landed solidly on Mark. A look somewhere between apprehension and amazement filled his expression. "But when I got that call from Alicia—" He drew a shaky breath. "How could I not want to meet my son?"

Mark had to bite the inside of his cheek to keep from blurting out he had no use for another father. Lindsey's tension was palpable, even to Shadow, who crept closer and pushed his nose under her hand.

"Well, you've met me now," he stated brusquely. "But if you're looking for us to have some kind of relation-ship, forget it."

Owen directed a frown toward Lindsey. "Guess I shouldn't be surprised you poisoned him against me. Audra had plenty to say, too, I imagine."

"*Poisoned?*" Lindsey bristled. "We only told him the truth."

"I admit I made mistakes. Serious ones I'll regret for the rest of my life."

Lindsey swiped at her cheeks. "Like walking out on Mom and me? Like turning your back on the ranch your parents built from scratch and that Audra and I have worked so hard to keep in the family?"

"Yeah. All of the above…" His voice faded as his gaze met Mark's. He abruptly tore his eyes away. "And more."

Oddly, Mark experienced a stab of sympathy for the man. "You really loved my mother, didn't you?"

"I did. And if I'd only fought for her——" Owen clenched his jaw. "I'm sorry, Lindsey. I know how that sounds. Please believe how much I love you. I may have married your mom for the wrong reasons, but I'll never regret having you as my daughter."

"Then why did you act like it for so many years?"

"Because I was a selfish jerk. I realize it's too little, too late, but after our blowup last year over the ranch stuff, I had some hard thinking to do. A few months ago, I started going to church again, and I've been seeing the pastor for counseling." Owen inched closer to her. "I have a lot more work to do on myself, but I'm trusting in God's forgiveness, and I'm hoping—praying—that someday you'll be able to forgive me, too." He glanced up at Mark and added, "Both of you."

Church? Prayer? Forgiveness? Unable to choke out a coherent reply, Mark waved a hand. "Excuse me."

Moments later, he stood in the backyard while trying to draw a full breath. Could faith make that big a difference in someone's messed-up life?

Lost in thought, he startled when a wet nose brushed his hand. He reached down to rub Shadow's ears.

The porch screen door clicked shut behind Lindsey. She came up beside him. "You okay?"

He straightened and shoved his hands into his jeans pockets. "Not sure. It's a lot to take in."

"Which part?"

"Meeting him. Hearing him admit his mistakes and regrets."

Lindsey sighed. "Wanting to believe he's really changed."

He faced her. "Do you buy it?"

"I don't know yet." She nodded toward the window over the barn, where they could see Samuel waltzing with baby Sophie in his arms. "Now there's an example of a man who came back to the Lord and truly became a better person."

"So you're saying anything's possible."

"With God, yes. With me?" She completed the thought with a helpless shrug.

The rumble of a car engine drew Mark's attention. Owen was just driving away. "Is he heading back to Oklahoma already?"

"Not yet. He wants to clear the air with Audra, too. Honestly, Mark, I'm starting to think he's sincere." Lindsey sank into the nearest Adirondack chair. "One thing I know for certain, though—my withholding forgiveness hurts me a lot more than it hurts him."

Her statement struck an unpleasant chord in him. Because clinging to his bitterness toward God certainly hadn't done a thing to ease his pain over losing Kellie. It had only made everything about the months and years that followed that much harder.

*   *   *

Over the next couple of weeks, Mark had several more phone conversations with his parents, who both seemed to think Owen deserved a chance.

"Your loyalty means the world to me," his dad said at one point, "but Owen McClement is your flesh and blood. I'm not saying he has to be your new best friend, but try putting yourself in his shoes for a minute. You know as well as anyone how life's curve balls can send you in directions you never could have anticipated."

While he chewed on that, he had the building sites to oversee—his own included, now that he was weatherizing the cabin and arranging for power and water supplies. On top of everything else, he'd been working with Uncle Hank, Audra and Lindsey to navigate the legal procedures involved in setting up the conservancy. Some days, it seemed he spent more time in meetings or on the phone than on the job.

It was the second week of February before it dawned on him how much time had passed since he'd talked to Holly, much less arranged time in his schedule for Davey. Neither of them had been far from his thoughts, though, and with the weekend coming up, maybe he could make amends.

On Thursday morning, while monitoring progress at the event center, he kept an eye out for Holly. She typically arrived at the ranch around eight thirty, after dropping Davey at school, and today she was right on schedule. He lingered at the job site until he saw her walking from her van to the back porch. She looked amazing this morning in jeans and a pine green turtleneck sweater, her brown waves brushing her shoulders. Pulse ramping up, he jogged over.

She looked his way with an uncertain smile. "Mark, hi. How…is everything?"

"Busy." He clenched his jaw. "For which I have to apologize. Again."

"I know you've been busy." She did a terrible job of disguising her eye roll. "I meant, how are *you*?"

A much harder question to answer. Maybe a little humor would help. "I try not to think about it too much. It gives me a headache."

Lips pursed, she marched up the porch steps, then turned with a frustrated sigh. "I'm sorry, but I'm running low on tolerance for people who don't know how to give an honest answer. Or worse, who change from cold to warm to cold again faster than Texas weather."

He gulped. "Holly—"

"I know you've had a lot of personal stuff to deal with since you came to the ranch, on top of all the emotional baggage you brought with you, and I've tried to be understanding and patient. But I have a little boy to consider, and his grades are continually slipping because he just doesn't seem to care anymore." She huffed out a breath. "So nothing else really matters to me right now except my son and my job, which I need to get to at the moment, so if you'll excuse me—"

"Please, Holly, wait." His stomach was churning worse than it had the morning he hadn't been able to make it to church. "I'm guilty of everything you said, but I *do* care. I've been saving this weekend for Davey, hoping to make up for lost time. I could talk to him about his attitude, maybe help him catch up with his schoolwork."

She shook her head. "I've made other plans. Since it's almost Valentine's Day and we have a big event scheduled, Davey will be spending the weekend with his grandparents in Dallas."

The news hit Mark like a punch to the gut. "Does he have to? He could stay with me at the cabin."

"It's already arranged. The Elliots are driving down tomorrow to take him back with them after school." She set her hand on the doorknob. "Sorry, I need to get inside. We have a lot to do before Saturday."

Disappointment squeezed his heart. Even after she'd stepped into the kitchen and firmly shut the door, he stood there staring for several long moments. His hopes for spending the weekend with Davey were shattered. He'd even missed the chance to ask Holly if she'd applied yet for her tearoom start-up loan.

A shout from his foreman drew his attention. "Hey, Mark! We need you over here, pronto!"

Giving himself a mental shake, he hurried back to the building site. "What's up, Pete?"

"One of the guys cut himself real bad. Can you drive him to the emergency clinic?"

The injured man was already striding toward Mark's truck, a blood-soaked towel wrapped around his hand. Mark flung open the passenger door. "Get in. Let's go."

Job-site accidents happened, but why now? Though Mark felt bad for the guy, there'd be insurance claims to deal with, plus the crew would be down a man—and they were already shorthanded since a couple of workers had come down with the flu last week. If Mark had to tell the River Bend Events ladies he couldn't complete their building on schedule, they wouldn't be happy.

And he couldn't bear making Holly any more upset with him than she already was.

* * *

Holly kept it to herself that Mark had invited Davey to the cabin for the weekend. Her son would gladly have chosen Mark and Shadow over his paternal grandparents, but the Elliots deserved time with their grandson. Besides, sending Davey to Dallas for a couple of days gave his grandparents what they wanted while letting Holly off the hook for another uncomfortable visit.

The weekend probably wouldn't do much for Davey's attitude, though. She made sure he took his school assignments along and reminded him that when he returned Sunday evening, she'd be checking to see how much of his homework he'd completed. Now, if only she could count on the Elliots to make sure he actually unzipped his backpack and cracked a book at least once.

River Bend Events had been hired for the Gabriel Bend Lions Club Valentine's party, held at the city's community center, and it went off without a hitch. Since Valentine's Day was also Spencer and Lindsey's first wedding anniversary, the couple left on Sunday morning for a couple of days at the coast, which left Holly and Joella to handle the after-party accounting and cleanup.

Holly agreed to meet her in-laws halfway to bring Davey home, so they designated a Mexican restaurant along I-35 in Waco. By the time Holly arrived that evening, the exhausting weekend and typically horrendous freeway traffic had taken their toll. She managed the appropriate smiles and nods while Davey and his grandparents described their excursions to the aquarium, a miniature golf course and the Perot Museum of Nature and Science. Holly didn't even need to ask if Davey had gotten around to his schoolwork.

While her son finished his dessert of sopapillas drenched in honey, Holly ordered a large coffee to go for the drive back to Gabriel Bend. The sugar had Davey wound up—probably a culmination of all the treats his grandparents had filled him with over the past two days—so he chattered most of the way home. That, plus the coffee, helped keep her alert, but she worried she wouldn't get him settled down enough for a good night's sleep.

Then, shortly after 4:30 a.m., Davey's seizure alarm went off. Holly jolted awake and stumbled to his room. She couldn't do much more than watch over and comfort him, and thankfully the seizure passed quickly, but each time her son experienced one of these episodes, it broke her heart a little bit more.

When awareness returned, he mumbled, "My head hurts, Mom."

"I know, honey." She pulled him into her arms. "It'll be okay. I've got you."

Knowing she'd never relax enough to catch one last hour of sleep, she guided Davey to the living room sofa, where she could keep an eye on him, and covered him with an afghan. While he dozed, she quietly made herself a toasted English muffin and a cup of Earl Grey, then settled at the dinette with her Bible and book of daily devotions.

The reading from First Corinthians brought a lump to Holly's throat: *But as it is written, Eye hath not seen, nor ear heard, neither have entered into the heart of man, the things which God hath prepared for them that love him.*

"What are you telling me, God?" she whispered. "My world seems so bound up in just getting through *today* that I can't even think about what the future may hold."

And yet she'd forged ahead with her business plan for the tearoom, and now Mrs. Skinner at Riverside State

Bank had her loan application in hand. Since meeting with the woman early last week, Holly had tried to put the application out of her mind. She had no business even attempting such a grand plan at this point in her life, much less getting her hopes up that it could actually happen.

It's all your fault, Mark Caldwell. If you hadn't inquired about the vacant shop and encouraged me to dream again...

At the memory of how curt she'd been with him the other morning, her stomach flipped. True, she'd been stressed over preparations for the Lions Club party, but he had all kinds of pressures in his life, too, and he didn't deserve her snapping at him.

Even if he did keep disappointing Davey. And that part was a little harder to forgive.

By the time the first rays of sun crept through the blinds, Holly had decided to keep her boy home from school. He was sleeping soundly now, his soft snores reminding her of a kitten's purr. She texted Joella to tell her about Davey's seizure and to say she wouldn't be coming out to the ranch.

An hour or so later, Davey stirred and said he was hungry. While he sipped a glass of orange juice, Holly found something soothing to watch on HGTV, then started a pan of oatmeal on the stove. She added Davey's favorites—cinnamon, raisins, dried cranberries, chopped walnuts and a dash of brown sugar.

As she carried the bowl to her son, her cell phone rang. She handed Davey his oatmeal, then answered the call without checking the display.

"Is Davey okay?" It was Mark, sounding slightly frantic. "Joella said he had a seizure in the middle of the night."

"He's fine. He slept it off and is having breakfast now."

"Good. I was worried."

Despite the unpleasantness from a few days earlier, she was touched that Mark had reached out to check on Davey. "I appreciate you calling, Mark. Really, he's okay." Yawning, Holly sank down on a chair at the dinette. The short night was catching up with her. "What with his grandparents providing nonstop entertainment all weekend, plus way too much sugar, he probably just got a little overstimulated."

"Are you taking him to see his doctor?"

"I'll let her know about the seizure, but she'll just remind me it's par for the course with an epileptic child."

He released a groan. "I hate he has to go through this."

"Me, too." Holly rested her forehead in her hand. "Mark, about how I spoke to you the other day…"

"Please. Don't worry about it."

"But I do. I feel awful for not being more understanding about everything you've had to deal with these last few months. If I'd—"

The call-waiting tone beeped in her ear. She lowered the phone to see whom the incoming call was from. Reading Riverside State Bank on the display, she sucked in a breath. "Um, Mark, I need to take this other call."

"Okay, tell Davey I'm thinking about him. And let me know if I can do anything to help."

"I will. Thanks."

Switching calls, she could barely suppress the butterflies swarming her stomach and keep her voice level. "H-hello? Holly Elliot speaking."

"This is Miriam Skinner from the bank. We have a

decision on your loan application. Could you come in to meet with me this afternoon?"

Holly glanced at Davey, who'd finished his oatmeal and was mindlessly flipping TV channels. "I—I don't know. My son is home sick from school today."

"Oh, that's too bad." Mrs. Skinner sighed. "Unfortunately, I'm leaving town tomorrow on family business and won't be back for several days. Is it possible someone could stay with your son for an hour or so?"

"Maybe. I'll ask a friend if she can come over."

"Let me know what you work out. I'll be here until four thirty."

Holly thanked the woman and disconnected. She made a few calls, but everyone was tied up with other things. Oh, well, if Davey perked up enough in the next couple of hours, she could take him with her. It wasn't as if he had anything contagious.

How had life gotten so complicated? If she'd stayed in Waxahachie, she'd still be running her very *un*complicated home-based catering service. It would never have made her rich by any stretch of the imagination, but with a few years' worth of savings padded by Blaine's life insurance benefits, she'd been able to provide for her son.

She laid the phone aside and rested her head atop her folded hands. It was no use looking back on the life she could never return to. As for the future…at the moment, she was too tired to care.

"You mean… I didn't qualify?" Chest throbbing, Holly stared at the gray-haired loan officer across the desk from her.

"I'm so sorry, Mrs. Elliot, but the underwriters don't feel there's enough in your favor to justify the risk."

Mrs. Skinner tapped coral-pink nails on the open folder in front of her. "Your credit score is a little lower than we'd like—"

"But I always pay my bills on time."

"Yes, but you're also a partner in a business venture with an outstanding construction loan."

Holly shouldn't be surprised that the new event center had factored in the bank's decision. "We fully expect the increased income our building generates to easily offset the cost."

"That, of course, remains to be seen." The woman went on to enumerate other reasons Holly's loan application was being denied. Though her tone was kind and her expression sympathetic, she gave no opening for an appeal. "Again, I'm very sorry we couldn't help you. Perhaps in another year or two…"

Unable to speak, Holly could only nod. She pushed up from the chair and hurried out of the office before the tears flowed.

"Mom?" Looking much more alert than he had that morning, Davey rose from the sofa where she'd left him in the lobby. "Aren't you gonna get the tearoom?"

"Not now, hon." Managing a weak smile, she reached for his hand. "Let's go home, okay?"

"But Mark was so sure—"

"Well, he was wrong."

Why, why, *why* had she set herself up for yet another disappointment? Hadn't she learned her lesson about the dangers of dreaming? If she'd never happened upon the vacant shop, if she hadn't glimpsed those nosegays painted on the window glass, if Mark hadn't contacted the leasing agent and her friends hadn't pushed her about the business plan and loan application…

It was a good thing their apartment was only a short

drive from downtown, because she could barely see through her tears. Davey kept patting her arm and handing her fistfuls of tissues, and when they got home, he made her curl up under an afghan in her favorite chair while he made her a cup of chamomile tea.

She accepted his offering with a loud sniff. "Thank you, sweetie. What would I do without you?"

"I'll always be here for you, Mom, just like you always are for me." He kissed the top of her head. "You should take a nap. I'll be in my room if you need anything, okay?"

Napping in the middle of the day wasn't usually her style, but she couldn't escape the physical and emotional fatigue creeping up on her. After a few sips of tea, she set the mug on the side table and cuddled deeper beneath the afghan. Behind her, she heard Davey rustling about in the kitchen area, and then his bedroom door closed.

He was right. They had each other, and they didn't need anyone else. Yes, it had been hard—excruciatingly hard—after Blaine died, but they'd managed. Day by day, they'd managed.

This is the day which the Lord hath made...this is the day...

"Holly? Holly, wake up."

The voice pulled her out of a deep sleep. "Blaine?"

"No. It's Mark." His thumb slid across something wet on her cheek. "Wake up, Holly. You're dreaming."

Dreaming—that's what had gotten her into this mess. She sat up and shook herself. When her vision cleared, she saw Mark kneeling beside her chair, his forehead etched with concern.

She clutched the afghan. "What are you doing here?"

"Davey used your phone to text me. I came as soon as I got out of my meeting."

Dumbfounded, she glanced around for her son, who stood a few steps behind Mark. "Davey—"

"I had to, Mom. I thought he could help."

"He was scared for you," Mark said. "He told me you were really upset after the loan was denied." He laid his hand on her arm. "If I'd known you were seeing the bank officer today—"

"What? You'd have ridden in on your white horse to rescue me? Well, I don't need rescuing." Tossing the afghan aside, she lurched to her feet. "It's been an exhausting few days, that's all, and I wasn't expecting to get the loan anyway, so it's no great loss."

Standing up so quickly had made her light-headed. She stumbled against Mark, who rose to steady her. "Take it easy," he said softly. "Let me get you some water or something."

"I'm okay." She pushed against his solid chest until she found her footing, then dropped her hands to her sides and tried to smile. "It was kind of you to stop by but completely unnecessary. I'm sorry Davey bothered you."

"It's no bother. I—I care, Holly. And I feel awful for you, and somehow responsible."

"No, no, of course you're not responsible." And yet before she'd fallen asleep, she'd been ready to blame him and everyone else because *she'd* been foolish enough to hope for the impossible.

Shrugging, he stuffed his hands into his pockets. "I just wish I could fix this for you."

Why did he have to stand there looking the picture of compassion and yet so handsomely helpless? It would be all too easy to let her guard down, but she couldn't. She needed to find her own strength, for her sake and for Davey.

Sidling past him, she opened the door to the landing. "I'm very grateful for your concern, but we'll be fine. You should go."

"Are you sure there isn't—"

"Very sure." She forced herself to meet his gaze with a smile. "Goodbye, Mark."

Jaw clenched, hurt in his eyes, he strode out.

"Mo-om!" Davey glared at her. "Why are you always so mean to him? Now he'll prob'ly never invite me to his cabin again!" He spun around and ran to his room. The slam of his door shook the whole apartment.

Drained, Holly collapsed into a kitchen chair. Her son was right. The man did tend to provoke powerful emotional responses in her—which too often led to words and actions she later regretted. This couldn't be good for either one of them, and it certainly wasn't how a friend should be treated.

Or maybe she was deliberately keeping Mark at arm's length. Because if she ever let him become something more than a friend, the risk of having yet another dream dashed might be more than her heart could bear.

Chapter Twelve

Mark left Holly's apartment in a haze of confusion. What was it with the two of them that they couldn't seem to maintain a civil friendship? True, he'd gotten off on the wrong foot with her from day one—all his fault. Well, mostly. But why this ongoing emotional seesaw?

He could almost hear Kellie's voice in his head: *"You just have to try harder, Daddy. Love is worth fighting for."*

Could he really be falling in love with Holly? Or was he confusing his affection for Davey with romantic feelings for the boy's mom?

A slow-moving green tractor loomed on the country road ahead. He braked and swerved, narrowly avoiding a rear-end collision. That's what he got for letting his mind wander to places it didn't need to be going.

Back at the ranch, he checked in briefly with each of his site foremen, then stopped by the house for Shadow and told Aunt Lois he'd be spending the night at the cabin.

"Don't you want to eat first?" she asked. "Supper will be on the table in half an hour."

Savory aromas from the oven teased his senses but

barely tweaked his appetite. "If it's okay with you, I'll just make myself a sandwich and eat it later. Right now, I'm craving some peace and quiet."

Sympathy warmed her gaze. "You've been running yourself ragged lately, haven't you?"

He answered with a half-hearted lift of a shoulder.

Twenty minutes later, he parked the truck outside the cabin. While Shadow made his usual circuit to sniff out any lurking critters, Mark lit a fire in the potbelly stove, then filled the dog's bowl with kibble and refreshed his water.

With his work boots off and his feet propped on the opposite chair, he settled in to read through the conservancy paperwork from this afternoon's meeting. The plans were coming together, and this was too important to let anything fall through the cracks.

By the next morning, he was thinking much more clearly—or so he told himself. He needed to stay focused on what mattered. Number one, completing the event center and Samuel's house on time. Number two, making the conservancy a reality. And number three, following through with his commitment to mentor Davey. No reason he couldn't spend quality time with the boy while keeping his interactions with Holly to a minimum.

Much safer for both of them.

He gave her a few days' grace to get over Monday's disappointment. Then, at the McClement ranch on Thursday afternoon, he ambled over as she strode out to her minivan.

When she turned toward him with those amazing green eyes, his tongue plastered itself to the roof of his mouth and his brain slipped out of gear.

So much for his plan to keep his guard up around Holly...

She cocked her head. "Hi. Did you need something?"

He unstuck his tongue and forced a swallow. "I wondered if Davey has plans for Saturday. I'm free in the afternoon, and I thought we could do something together."

"I'm not sure." She pulled her lower lip between her teeth. "I mean, we haven't made specific plans, but after last weekend, I've been trying to keep things low-key."

"He hasn't had another seizure, I hope?"

"No, but I don't want to take any chances." She edged closer to her van. "I have to go. School will be out soon."

"Holly, wait. If saying no is about me butting into your life, I promise it won't happen again. I just want to be there for Davey."

Looking away, she shook her head. "I know you mean well, Mark. But I'm afraid asking you to spend time with my son was a mistake."

His gut clenched. "Why would you say that?"

"Because I'm his only parent, and it's up to me to protect him. Me and no one else."

He scoffed. "Is there some law that says you have to do it alone?"

"No, but Davey needs security, stability. He needs to know whom he can count on." She pulled open the van door and set her tote inside. Still with her back to him, she murmured, "And I've realized I'm the only one who can give him that."

So it was more than about Mark interfering in her life, or even the times he'd missed making plans with Davey. It was the possibility that once his year was up—maybe even sooner—he wouldn't be staying in Gabriel Bend.

"It's true," he said. "At this point I don't know how

long I'll be around. But I told you before, I don't renege on commitments, professional or otherwise. If, somewhere down the road, I do decide to go back to Montana, I give you my word that I will not leave Davey high and dry."

She pivoted, the fire in her eyes searing every inch of his face. "How can you make such a promise? And what does that even mean?"

Backing up a step, he plowed his fingers through his hair. "I don't know, okay? I'd figure out something. Just don't—" His voice broke. "Don't keep me away from Davey. Please. I—I need him."

Her lips parted. Two tiny vertical lines formed between her scrunched-up brows. For the briefest moment, her expression softened into a look of compassion—or so he wanted to believe.

Abruptly, she climbed into the van and fumbled with the ignition key. "I need to think," she muttered before pulling the door closed. She mouthed the words again as she buckled her seat belt and started the engine.

A moment later, she drove away.

Now he'd blown it. Really, really blown it. Practically *begging* her for time with her son? *You don't know when to quit, do you, Caldwell?*

Way to go, Holly.

"It's up to me to protect him. Me and no one else." Talk about helicopter parenting!

And it wasn't like she'd been such a marvelous mom lately. Most days she felt like an utter failure. Learning to navigate life as a young widow had been scary enough, but as the sole parent of an active boy with special needs, how could she afford to refuse any help offered?

Before she pulled into the after-school pickup queue, she'd made up her mind to let Davey spend Saturday with Mark. While she waited in line, she texted him. If the offer still stands, I'll bring Davey out Saturday afternoon. What time works for you?

A few seconds later, the blinking dots indicated Mark had read the message and was typing a reply.

Then…nothing.

The driver behind her tapped the horn, and Holly looked up to see the line of cars had advanced. She waved in her rearview mirror and inched forward. As an aide opened the passenger door for Davey, Holly checked her phone once more. Still no response from Mark. He must have had to deal with a construction issue or something.

Continuing out of the drive-through, she smiled and asked, "Hey, hon, how was your day?"

Davey heaved a noisy sigh. "I had to sit in the principal's office for thirty minutes."

"What? Why?" Holly tried to keep her cool as she entered traffic.

"I got upset and used a bad word. I have a note I'm supposed to give you."

Breathe…just breathe… "It sounds like you deserved your time-out, but I have to pay attention to my driving right now, so we'll talk about it after we get home."

Maybe it was just as well Mark hadn't replied to her text. Allowing her son to spend Saturday with him and Shadow after he'd acted out at school—yet again— might seem like a reward.

On the other hand, Davey's repeated misbehavior could mean he needed Mark's positive influence all the more. She couldn't deny the promising changes she'd observed in her son when Mark had been more consistent about spending time with him.

That was the problem, though—consistency. More accurately, the lack thereof. If she had any sense, she'd permanently write Mark out of their lives and ask Spencer or Samuel if one of them could spare even an hour or two each week to mentor Davey. They surely weren't any busier than Mark.

And neither of them was even considering leaving Gabriel Bend.

At the apartment, Holly sat Davey at the table with a glass of milk and apple slices while she read the note from the teacher. Apparently, Davey had failed a math test and one of his classmates had teased him about it. He'd gotten angry, called the boy an ugly name and used a mild obscenity. Holly hated to imagine where he'd picked up such a word—certainly not from anyone among her acquaintances. She'd better increase her vigilance about his video games and TV programs.

After a stern lecture and taking away his screen time for the next few days, she sat down with him to review the answers he'd missed on his test. It didn't take long to determine he knew perfectly well how to work the problems. He'd just been lazy and careless.

As they were finishing, her phone chimed with an incoming text. She'd all but forgotten about waiting for Mark to reply. Seeing his name and number on the screen, she carried the phone to the other side of the room before opening the message. You were right. This was a mistake. I'm the wrong guy to be mentoring your son. I hope you find someone else.

Ridiculously, her heart plummeted.

"Who was it, Mom?" Davey asked from his seat at the table.

"Nothing important." Dredging up a smile, she stuffed the phone into her jeans pocket. "Do you have any other homework for tomorrow?"

He stretched one arm across the table and laid his head down with a dramatic groan. "A dumb grammar worksheet, and I'm supposed to read a chapter in my boring science book."

"Better get busy, then."

So much for Mark's *needing* to spend time with Davey. If she had any lingering doubts about his reliability as a mentor, his callous text had just confirmed them.

Well, she'd just think of something fun she and her son could do together this weekend. Maybe a movie or bowling or miniature golf.

Right. Nothing a ten-year-old boy liked better than being seen in public hanging out with his mom.

Over the next couple of weeks, life for Holly settled into a more predictable rhythm. Not necessarily a comfortable one, but it was manageable. She attended to River Bend Events business during the day, then focused on mom duties and homework supervision after picking up Davey from school. He'd finally stopped asking when he'd get to see Mark and Shadow again, but though his attitude had become less turbulent, his increasing apathy was troubling.

February slipped into March, and with cooperation from the weather, progress on the event center proceeded on schedule. Joella had decided they should hold a grand opening for the center upon its completion and publicize the event widely, not only in Gabriel Bend but throughout the county and beyond. The open house would allow them to showcase both the facility and the services they offered, including Holly's cooking and catering talents.

Planning the grand opening, plus preparing for and hosting their currently scheduled functions, meant Holly had little time for anything else—least of all, fretting over the tattered remains of her friendship with Mark. Besides, she heard he'd been plenty busy, too. As word spread about the new general contractor in town, he'd been hired for various remodeling projects, along with building a new house for Mayor Nicolson's family. And all this on top of his ongoing efforts to establish what would be called the Hands and Heart Nature Preserve. The name memorialized the bygone partnership between Arturo Navarro and Egan McClement, *Rancho de Manos y Corazón*—Hands and Heart Ranch.

On a breezy Monday morning in late March, Holly stood out front at the McClement house. With Joella and Lindsey unavailable, she'd been left to supervise as the rental company packed up the party pavilion, tables and chairs, and other equipment following a small wedding and reception on Saturday. She glanced toward the new building and gave silent thanks that soon all these extra rental arrangements would be unnecessary.

A motion at the road caught her eye, and she recognized Mark's truck turning up the driveway. He slowed as he came even with the porch, then pulled off to the side, got out and started her way.

For no good reason, her breath hitched. It wasn't as if she hadn't seen or spoken with him in the past few weeks—she'd been over to the event center on a number of occasions to check the progress and address issues that arose. Of course, Lindsey or Joella had usually gone along, too, and often the foreman or other workers had also been in on the discussions.

Now, there was no one else around except the rental company crew, and they were too busy to be any distraction at all.

"Sorry to bother you." Mark removed his hat as he approached. He'd taken to wearing a tan straw Stetson like Spencer's, only his looked a lot newer. "I'm looking for Audra or Lindsey."

So he hadn't stopped on her account after all. How could she feel so disappointed? "They're busy with calves. It's that time of year."

"Ah. Right." He pinched the crown of his hat, then settled it low on his brow. "I'll catch them later. Thanks."

"Is there something I could help you with?"

"Not really. I had an idea to run by them about the conservancy." He turned to go.

She suddenly wished he wouldn't rush off, that somehow they could clear the air between them. "I could deliver a message for you. I mean, in case you're not around when they get back."

"That's okay, nothing urgent." Once more, he turned, then hesitated, his gaze locked on something in the distance. "Do you mind if I ask how Davey's doing?"

"He's…" She wished she could say her son was fine, but she couldn't bring herself to shade the truth. "He's been—"

"Ma'am?" The driver of the rental truck strode over, clipboard in hand. "We're all done. Just need your signature."

Secretly relieved by the interruption, she took the clipboard and signed the receipt, then accepted the customer copy. "Thank you so much."

The man nodded across the driveway. "Your new building looks great. We'll miss doing business with you."

"I'm sure we'll be calling on you again as needs arise. And watch for an invitation to our open house next month."

As the man climbed into his truck, Mark drew her attention again. He cocked his head. "Open house?"

"Yes, to celebrate the grand opening of the event center." Hesitating, she narrowed one eye. "There's no reason to be concerned it won't be completed on time, is there?"

"No, we're right on schedule." He tapped his hat brim. "Gotta get back to work. Have a nice day."

Have a nice day?

Watching him go, she recalled every single reason he so thoroughly infuriated her. For starters, he was moody and meddling and morose. Not to mention the massive chip he carried on his shoulder.

But he was also incredibly kind and caring, even if he didn't always show it in the best way. As for his agreement to mentor Davey, *she* was the one who'd initially reneged on that arrangement, not Mark.

Who are you really trying to protect, Holly Elliot? Your son...or yourself?

After a long day of checking on each of the projects he had going, Mark arrived at the ranch beneath an orange-and-purple sky. It didn't quite compare with Montana's Big Sky sunsets, but he couldn't complain.

In fact, there wasn't a lot he could complain about these days. Since he'd taken over construction of the event center and Samuel's house from Jay Graham, the man had continued to send business Mark's way. Additional referrals kept him flush with jobs, and the steady income helped pay for improvements to the old cabin. Now that it was cozy and comfortable, he and Shadow had moved in. And the better acquainted he grew with the ranch and both sides of his Texas family, the more Gabriel Bend had begun to feel like home.

Something was missing, though—that, he couldn't deny. He suspected Shadow was feeling it, too. Making friends with Davey had sparked new life in the dog, but lately he'd grown lethargic, no longer showing the slightest bit of interest in his favorite game of fetch or sniffing out critters in the underbrush around the cabin. Mark only hoped the old boy wasn't getting sick. Maybe he should make a veterinary appointment.

When he stopped at the house to pick up Shadow, he found Audra, Spencer and Lindsey there. It looked as if they'd just finished having dinner with Uncle Hank and Aunt Lois.

"We heard you were looking for us this morning," Audra said. "Something about the conservancy?"

Before he could answer, Aunt Lois ushered him to the table and set a steaming bowl of beef stew in front of him. "Get some food in your belly, young man. You can talk while you eat."

"I told you, you don't have to feed me every day. I do know how to cook for myself." The aroma was already tickling his taste buds, though, and he couldn't resist a big mouthful.

Lindsey sipped her iced tea. "So what's on your mind, big brother?"

She'd started calling him that recently, but he still wasn't used to it, and his heart gave a happy little flip. All through childhood, he'd wished he had siblings, and now he had a sister.

He swallowed another bite, then dabbed his mouth with a napkin. "I wanted to ask about those piles of stones at the entrance to your driveway."

"The footings for the old ranch gate?" Audra heaved a sad sigh. "They've become an eyesore, but I've never had the heart to tear them down."

Mark had seen photos of the original gate. The one he liked best showed Arturo and Egan arm in arm, standing proudly between the stone and cedar pillars. *Rancho de Manos y Corazón* had been burned into the arched wooden crosspiece overhead.

"What would you think," he began, "if we used those stones to recreate the gate as the entrance to our nature preserve?"

Audra's eyes welled. Gripping Lindsey's hand, she briskly nodded her approval. "I love the idea. Hank, would it be all right with you?"

"Absolutely. We can make it a family project."

They talked more about the plan while Mark finished his meal. Afterward, as he prepared to head to the cabin with Shadow, Spencer walked out with him. "If it's okay with you, I'll pop in on Samuel and Joella and fill them in."

"That'd be great. I'm about talked out for the night." He opened his truck door for Shadow to jump inside.

"Hard to miss how busy you've been lately. Several new clients, so I hear." Leaning against the side of the truck, Spencer didn't look in any hurry to get upstairs to the barn apartment. "Kinda looks like you're settling in for the long haul."

Mark shrugged. "Maybe I am. Jay Graham's ready to retire and asked me to think about taking over his construction company."

"Wow. That does sound permanent. What about your business in Missoula?"

"My foreman's ready to buy me out. We've already started the paperwork."

With a thoughtful grimace, Spencer scratched the back of his head. "A lot of big decisions. I hope you've been praying about them, because any plan that doesn't align with God's will doesn't stand much chance of success."

Shadow whined, and Mark reached inside the truck to scratch the dog's head. "What is it, boy? Are you trying to tell me my cousin's right?" His shoulders sagged. "Truth is, I've been trying to pray more. I know it's what Kellie would have wanted. But I'm afraid—" He clamped his lips together.

"Afraid of what?" Spencer asked softly.

"I'm afraid even if I pray and get everything else right, God still won't grant me the one thing I need most."

"You think our God is so hardhearted that He'd deny His children any good thing?"

Mark glared at his cousin. "He denied me my daughter's life."

Exhaling sharply, Spencer looked toward the darkened sky. "I don't know why God didn't allow you more time with Kellie. But I believe with all my heart that her life, short as it was, had meaning. Try focusing on how the Lord blessed you through your daughter instead of what you believe He took away."

"I know you're right, but it's hard. I feel like I've been angry for a long, long time. Angry at God, angry at myself that I couldn't do more." He braced his hands on the upper part of the door frame. "What if it's too late? What if I can't ever be—can't ever feel—"

"Normal?"

"*Worthy.*" Mark tiredly shook his head. "What if I can never feel worthy of the love and family I crave?"

Chapter Thirteen

Over the next several days, Holly noticed the stone bases on either side of the McClement ranch entrance had been shrinking. When she asked about it, Lindsey explained that the guys were moving them out to the conservancy easement and using them to build a memorial gate.

"It'll straddle the property line," Lindsey said, "and lanes from each ranch will merge at the entrance." Swiveling her laptop around on the worktable, she showed Holly the diagram. "This is entirely Mark's doing. He's thought of everything."

She nodded and smiled. "I'm glad for you. For both families."

With a pensive frown, Lindsey closed her laptop. "For a while there, I thought maybe you'd become the newest member of the Navarro-McClement clan."

Heat rushed up Holly's cheeks. "Where would you get an idea like that?"

"Possibly all the sparks flying between you and Mark? Except not so much lately. Seems like you two have been avoiding each other."

Holly made a pretense of riffling through her tote for something. "We've both been super busy lately."

"Uh-huh." Her friend folded her arms on the table and leaned in. "By my recollection, things started cooling about the time your loan for the tearoom was denied. Are you somehow blaming Mark?"

"The truth is, I blame myself for getting carried away and thinking it could really happen."

Joella entered the study just then. Dropping her things onto a chair, she glanced between Holly and Lindsey. "This looks like a serious discussion. I'd ask you to fill me in, but Mark just caught me outside. He'd like us to do another walk-through before they wrap things up."

"Yes!" Bouncing out of her chair, Lindsey threw one arm around Joella and extended the other toward Holly. "We're about to have our very own official event center!"

Her friends' excitement was contagious, and she joined in the group hug. No longer having to prepare her recipes in the church kitchen and then transport massive amounts of food to the ranch to serve their clients under party tents? How could she *not* be thrilled?

Shortly, they followed the grass-lined walkway up to the stone terrace outside the new building. In the rock-bordered beds on either side, landscapers worked to install creeping juniper, yaupon holly, sage and myrtle, all plants native to the Hill Country. These final touches truly made the center seem real.

Mark pushed open one of the double glass doors and motioned them through the vestibule. "Come on in and look around."

Holly entered last, eyes straight ahead as she brushed by him. A faint scent of construction dust mingled with his piney aftershave. As the door whispered shut, she sensed him come up beside her and stifled a shiver. The fact that he continually had this effect on her was unnerving.

Joella and Lindsey had moved a few steps ahead, their appreciative gazes sweeping the elegant banquet hall. Rustic wooden beams framed the white cathedral ceiling above a tile floor patterned like a river winding through rocky banks. The last time Holly had toured the building, she'd had to step around tools, drop cloths, paint buckets and construction debris. Swept clean now, the room was even more beautiful than she'd envisioned when Jay Graham had first presented the design sketches. She couldn't withhold a gasp.

"Like it so far?" Mark said near her ear.

"It's…it's breathtaking."

"Whenever you're ready, I'll show you the kitchen."

Holly spotted Lindsey and Joella stepping into the passageway leading to the office area. Would they have been so obvious as to leave her alone with Mark on purpose? Yep, probably so. She drew a quick breath and smiled at him. "Lead on."

The expansive kitchen was everything Holly had hoped for—stainless-steel work surfaces, spacious cabinets and walk-in pantry, an ideal arrangement for food prep, cooking, serving and cleanup.

"Appliances will be delivered and installed tomorrow," Mark said. "When they're done, I'll have you come over to check everything out."

Turning in a slow circle, she nodded. "This would have been so perfect for the quinceañera we're doing for the Garza twins on Saturday."

"Sorry we couldn't finish sooner, but we didn't want

to cut corners. You'll be all set for the grand opening in two weeks, though."

"Good. First thing Monday, we plan to mail invitations and begin publicizing the open house." Holly skimmed her hand along a stainless-steel counter. "Thank you for making this happen. If you hadn't been available to take over for Jay, who knows when—or if—our building would have been completed."

Turning away, he used his thumb to wipe away a smudge on a cabinet door. "I guess God knew what He was doing."

She blinked. Had she heard him correctly? "Mark, are you—"

Joella burst through the swinging doors, Lindsey right behind her. Cell phone in hand, Joella said, "The rental company just called. They had a scheduling issue and need to deliver everything for the Garza sisters' quinceañera a day early. They'll be here in an hour."

Thoughts churning, Holly palmed her forehead. "Are we ready for them? I don't think Spencer has even mowed yet."

"You're right," Lindsey said. "But he left early this morning to pick up three abandoned horses near Marble Falls. He took Samuel along, and they'll be gone for a while. I'd do it, but I'm supposed to be on calf duty with Audra."

Joella wrinkled her nose. "Unfortunately, I'm way behind on the party decorations—not to mention I know *nothing* about tractor mowers."

"Me, neither," Holly said. "Plus, I need to get to the church and start food prep. Is there someone else we could call?"

"Maybe one of the Navarro ranch hands," Lindsey suggested. "If they're not too busy with foals—"

Mark cleared his throat. "I can do the mowing."

"No." Holly firmly shook her head. "We couldn't ask."

"You didn't. I'm volunteering."

"We don't have time to argue—or refuse." Lindsey backed toward the door. "Holly, you know where we keep all the ranch keys. The one for the mower is on a ring with a squishy orange football. And thank you, Mark. You're a lifesaver!"

In the stark silence following her friends' departure, Holly strove to collect herself. "Okay, I'd better go get that key."

"Give me five minutes and I'll be right behind you."

By the time Holly had found the key, Mark was heading her way across the backyard. She pointed him toward the equipment shed and the big red tractor mower. "Are you sure this isn't keeping you from something more important?"

"Nothing that can't wait an hour. Where should I start?"

"The party pavilion will be erected out front—that's the most urgent. The rest can wait until Spencer gets back. I'm leaving for the church, but Joella's inside if you need anything."

Brow furrowed, Mark bounced the football key ring in his palm. "Holly...once things calm down a little, I was hoping we could...talk."

"Yes, me, too." She nodded slowly. "I mean, since we're bound to continue running into each other, I think we should try to clear the air."

"Right. Clear the air." His frown deepening, he edged away. "I'd better get started."

As he strode toward the equipment shed, Holly called, "Thank you again for mowing."

Without looking back, he lifted one hand in a curt wave.

She should have gone straight to her minivan and headed to the church, but she couldn't seem to get her feet moving. Had she somehow offended him—again? But how? After all, he'd brought up the suggestion of the two of them talking, and all she'd done was agree, because they did need to address whatever issues kept clouding the atmosphere between them.

Or maybe you already know what the problem is and don't want to admit it—don't want to admit you care for him more than your bruised heart ever imagined you could care for someone again.

Mark made quick work of mowing the front lawn. It was good to have something physical to do to take his mind off yet another awkward conversation with Holly. If only he could figure out how to fix whatever had gone wrong between them.

By the time the rental truck arrived, he'd moved on to the grassy strips along the driveway. While Joella supervised the pavilion setup, he continued past the house to mow the backyard and the area around the chapel. When he finished, he parked the tractor inside the equipment shed.

On his way to the house to return the key, he slowed as he neared the chapel doors. One door stood slightly ajar, like an invitation to enter. He hadn't worked up the nerve to attend an actual church service yet, but he'd been talking to God—really talking, not merely ranting—a lot more in the last couple of weeks. Weird thing was, he had the growing sense God was listening.

His breath quickening, he stepped through the door.

As his eyes adjusted to the dimness, he noticed a plastic crate sitting on the bench closest to the doors.

Fluffy pale-pink and white bows were piled inside, most likely to adorn the chapel for the quinceañera.

It struck him suddenly that Kellie would have turned fifteen on her last birthday. He'd never teach his daughter to drive, never get to intimidate her first boyfriend, never take a million photos of her before her senior prom, never walk her down an aisle like this one to meet her adoring groom...

"I don't understand, God." He spoke into the silence. "And I accept that I never will—in this life, anyway. But if You could help me find my way again, somehow help me be *happy* again—"

His voice broke. He sank onto a bench, his shoulders heaving with the tears he'd held in check since the day he'd buried his daughter.

Sometime later, hearing voices outside, he stood and hurriedly wiped his face on his sleeve. He peeked out the door and glimpsed Lindsey and Audra exiting the barn. Before he could duck out of sight, they saw him and detoured in his direction.

Audra's cheery smile abruptly turned to one of concern. She jogged over and cupped his cheek. "Oh, honey, you poor thing."

Sniffling, he released an embarrassed chuckle. "Who knew a few minutes in the chapel could open the floodgates?"

"I knew," she said with a nod. "In the weeks after Charles died, you could have mopped the floor three times a day with the buckets of tears I shed in there."

"I wish I'd known him better."

"He was the best uncle ever." Lindsey gave Audra a quick hug. "I'm going inside to clean up and make lunch. Mark, you're welcome to join us. By the way, the lawn looks great."

He handed her the tractor key. "Glad I could help. I'd better pass on lunch, though. I need to check on my jobs in town."

His route took him by the church, and when he saw Holly's van parked near the fellowship hall, his heart gave a little stutter. If she wasn't in the middle of cooking for Saturday's event, he'd go in there right now and *clear the air*, as she'd called it. Except for him, that meant telling her exactly how he felt, and as shaky as his emotions were after his breakdown in the chapel, he didn't think he could bear hearing her say she could never return his feelings.

And if, on top of shattering his newly defenseless heart, she never let him spend time with Davey again, he didn't know what he'd do.

Over the following week, Mark and his site foreman, Pete Castañeda, checked off the remaining items on the event center punch list. Tools and supplies had been cleared out, and the building had passed all required inspections. Now the cleaning crew was putting the final polish on the center.

"It's been great working with you, Pete." Mark shook the foreman's hand as they paused in one of the empty offices. "You've got a job with me anytime."

"Appreciate it. I was glad to hear you decided to stick around and take over Jay Graham's business."

"I only hope I can honor the fine reputation he's built in this community."

Pete grinned. "From my perspective, that won't be a concern."

Women's voices from the banquet room announced the arrival of Holly, Lindsey and Joella for their final walk-through. Heading out to greet them, Mark pasted on a smile and hoped he could keep his focus where it needed to be and not on how Holly's nearness made his pulse hammer. When she'd come in to see the new kitchen appliances a few days ago, he'd left Pete in charge and arranged to be busy elsewhere. But now that he'd made the decision to stay in Gabriel Bend, how long could he continue avoiding the conversation they needed to have?

As they went through each room, Joella and Lindsey buzzed with ideas for the open house while Holly jotted notes on her tablet. She didn't seem nearly as excited about the grand opening as her friends, but kept falling behind, as if her thoughts were elsewhere.

While Pete fielded Joella's and Lindsey's questions, Mark lingered near Holly. "You seem distracted. Is everything okay?"

"What? Oh, it's a hectic time, that's all." Her smile seemed forced.

Standing this close, Mark detected purple smudges beneath her eyes that makeup didn't quite conceal. "Are you sure that's all it is? Because—"

"Excuse me, I'd better catch up." She hurried after Lindsey and Joella, who'd circled back to the banquet hall.

If she wouldn't talk to him, there wasn't much he could do, but it didn't stop him from worrying.

After the walk-through, he accompanied the ladies to the house, where they completed the final paperwork and Lindsey handed him a check. In turn, he gave them the keys to the building and promised to take care of any problems that might arise in the coming weeks.

"Thank you so much, Mark." Lindsey gave him a hug. "You'll be at our grand opening, right?"

"I'm not sure." He cast an uneasy glance toward

Holly, who'd retreated to the window and still appeared lost in thought. "I need to make a trip to Missoula to wrap up my business there and bring some things back with me."

"But it can wait until afterward, can't it?" Lindsey had really perfected the persuasive little-sister pout.

He shrugged. "I'll see."

Abruptly, Holly turned from the window and scooped up her tote. "School will be out soon. I can't be late picking up Davey."

When she'd gone, Mark shook his head and muttered, "Something's not right."

"I agree," Joella said. "Holly hasn't been herself lately. She doesn't say much, but I get the feeling Davey's been giving her problems."

"What kind of problems? Has he had more seizures?"

"Not that Holly's mentioned," Lindsey replied. "But she brought him back after school the other day to work on grand opening plans, and they were definitely not getting along. I've never seen Davey so sullen and uncooperative, and Holly was on her last nerve."

Arms crossed, Joella leaned against the desk. "Mark, I thought you were mentoring Davey. What happened?"

"You'd have to ask Holly." He clenched his jaw and looked away. With a sigh, he continued softly, "I think I messed up one too many times."

Lindsey frowned. "Please tell me this isn't still about the tearoom. Because we're as guilty as you for getting her hopes up."

"I'm sure that's part of it." He released a ragged breath. "But the rest is…just me being me."

"Mark—" Lindsey began.

He lifted one hand. "No sympathy, okay? I've had

enough to last a lifetime. However, prayers for me to get my life back on track are needed and appreciated."

It was the morning of the grand opening, and Holly's brain felt like it could explode. Bad enough her careening thoughts had left her sleep-deprived most of the week, but today she was knocking heads with a ten-year-old who wanted to be anywhere but tagging along after his stretched-to-the-limit, short-tempered mom.

"This is an important day, Davey," she said as they headed out to the ranch. "You'll have to find something to occupy yourself while I get the food ready for this afternoon."

"But you keep grounding me from screens, so I can't even play my video games."

"I keep grounding you because you're ignoring your chores and aren't maintaining your grades." She harrumphed. "You play those games too much anyway. Dr. Liggett has warned you that certain ones can trigger seizures."

Arms locked across his chest, he mumbled, "Yeah, like that's ever happened."

It was true—she'd carefully researched the games she'd let him download, and so far there hadn't been any issues.

"It's not like you'd care anyway." Davey's tone wobbled. "Not like *anyone* cares."

She tore her gaze away from the road long enough to look at him in shock. "Don't say things like that. You *know* I care. I love you, Davey. You're my whole world."

Keeping his face averted, he replied with a snort.

She didn't have the energy for this—not today. *Just get me through the grand opening, Lord. Then I'll figure out what to do about my son.*

With the additional help they'd hired for the event, Holly quickly had her hands full getting the catering staff organized. As often as she could break away, she peeked into the small conference room, where she'd told Davey to stay. He'd brought the novel he'd been reading, and she'd also supplied him with a stack of the puzzle books he liked.

After a couple of hours, though, he'd grown restless and bored. "This is taking forever, Mom. Just let me play on your phone, okay?"

She pinched the bridge of her nose. This was her fault for not arranging for him to go to a friend's house for the day. Foolish to hope her son might actually *want* to participate in celebrating an occasion that meant so much to his mother and her friends.

Except she wasn't exactly in a celebratory mood. Whatever anticipation she'd once felt about the grand opening had been swallowed up by the stress of it all.

That, and her confusing feelings about Mark. No matter how hard she tried to put him out of her mind, it proved impossible.

"All right," she said, pulling her phone from her pocket. She handed it to Davey. "If someone calls, come find me."

"Sure." Stretched out on the carpeted floor, he was already searching the apps for the few games she kept on her phone.

Another hour went by. After a check of the buffet tables, Holly made a quick trip down the hall to look in on her son.

The room was empty.

She peeked into the adjoining office—also empty. After looking for him in the kitchen with no success, she knocked on the door of the men's restroom. "Davey? You in there?"

No answer.

Don't panic yet. He had to be here somewhere.

She returned to the banquet room, where she found Lindsey refastening a Mylar balloon that had come loose. "Hey, have you seen Davey?"

"Sorry, no. But I haven't exactly been watching for him." Lindsey called to Joella, who was adjusting a table centerpiece. "Has Davey been through here?"

"Not that I noticed." Joella strode over. "You can't find him?"

Holly released a shaky laugh. "I'm sure he's just exploring. But I told him not to go wandering around, and now it's like he just disappeared."

"Let's think this through." Lindsey took Holly's hand and gave it a calming pat. "If he isn't in the building, where's he most likely to go?"

There was only one answer. Sighing, Holly dipped her chin. "Probably to see Mark and Shadow."

"So call Mark and ask if Davey's over there."

Holly reached toward her pocket, then halted. "I can't. I gave Davey my phone to play games."

Joella quickly used her phone to place the call. "Hi, Mark. Davey wouldn't by chance be over there, would he?" She listened, then looked at Holly and shook her head. Voice lowered, she said, "He isn't even at home. He had a job to check on in town."

Holly's heart sank.

Joella returned to the call. "What? Okay, I'm putting her on."

Holly took the phone and pressed it to her ear. "Hello? Mark?"

"What's this about Davey being missing?"

"He's—" Her voice broke. "He's just…gone."

"Hang tight. I'm on my way."

Struggling to breathe, Holly thrust Joella's phone toward her. "He's coming. I should—"

"There you are, Holly." One of the kitchen helpers was marching toward her. "This is your phone, isn't it? I found it on the floor near the back exit."

Holly held out a trembling hand. "Yes. Thank you."

She gripped her phone and stared at it, as if it could tell her where her son had gone. The display showed her recent text messages—including the last ones she'd exchanged with Mark, which ended with him telling her he was the wrong guy to mentor her son.

"Oh, no. No, no, no…"

Lindsey touched her arm. "What is it?"

She showed her the messages. "I never meant for Davey to see these. I can't even imagine what he must be thinking right now."

This was her fault—all her fault. Why hadn't she deleted those texts?

And where could Davey have gone?

Dear God, please keep him safe. Please help us find him soon!

Chapter Fourteen

Lord, if You're hearing any of my prayers, let it be this one. Please, for Holly's sake, protect Davey and help us find him quickly.

Good thing there were no cops on the road, or they'd have ticketed Mark for driving well over the speed limit. On the way, he used the truck's hands-free phone link to call Aunt Lois.

"Davey's missing," he blurted. "Has he come by there?"

"No, I haven't seen him." Lois hesitated. "But it could explain something else. About an hour ago, Shadow was begging to go outside. He sniffed around the yard, then tore off across the pastures. I figured he was going back to the cabin, so I wasn't too concerned. Could he have sensed Davey out there somewhere?"

Knowing his dog, he didn't doubt it. "I'm heading that way. Just keep an eye out."

When he roared to a stop in front of the event center a few minutes later, Holly raced out to meet him.

He jogged around the truck. "Any sign of him yet?"

"Nothing. Mark, I'm so scared."

Instinctively, he drew her into his arms—something

he'd longed to do for weeks now, but never under such harrowing circumstances. "It's okay. We'll find him."

She stiffened and looked up at him. "He—he read our last texts."

His cryptic reply to her asking him to spend the afternoon with Davey was seared into his brain: "*You were right. This was a mistake.*" How many times had he reread that conversation and wished he could snatch back those words? He held her closer and kissed the top of her head. "I'm so sorry…"

She clung to him, her heart thudding against his chest. "We have to find him. We have to help him understand."

"We will, I promise." He guided her toward the truck and helped her into the passenger seat. "He couldn't have gotten far. He has to be somewhere on one of the ranches."

"Yes, but he's all alone, and—and anything could happen." Holly's pitch rose with each word. She clutched Mark's hand. "How will we ever find him?"

"I have some ideas. Besides, I don't think he's alone." He attempted a reassuring smile. "I'm pretty sure Shadow's with him."

"I pray you're right."

Behind the wheel again, Mark headed back to the road. He turned in at the Navarros' driveway, then skirted the barn and arena and aimed the truck down the lane toward the cabin. As the truck jounced along, they scanned the pastures on either side. A boy and a dog would be hard to spot if they'd wandered too far from the fence lines. The best Mark could hope for was that Davey had come looking for him to confront him about the text.

"Wait—stop!" Holly gripped the armrest, swiveling to look behind them as he braked. "I thought I saw something moving over that way."

Mark threw the truck into Reverse and backed up several feet. He peered through the windshield. "Where? What'd you see?"

After a moment, Holly's shoulders sagged. "It was probably just the wind in the grass."

They crept forward, Mark's gaze sweeping left and right as he steered. In the next pasture, he glimpsed the broken-down tree house where he'd first found Davey last fall. He'd warned the boy several times it wasn't a safe place to play, but...

He pulled alongside the gate and stopped. "I'm going to check something. Hang on a sec."

Striding to the fence, he detected no sign of movement around the tree. Then a furry black head popped up beyond a patch of bluebonnets. Shadow looked his way and gave a single bark.

Holly burst from the truck. "Davey?"

"Slow down." Mark stilled her hands as she tugged on the chain securing the gate. "If he's there, you don't want to scare him."

"But he could be hurt! I have to get to him."

He frowned at her pastel capris and flimsy sandals. "You're the one who's likely to get hurt if you go racing across rocks and thorny weeds dressed like that."

"I don't care. Let me through that gate right now!"

This was a fight Mark couldn't win. But he knew he'd feel the same way if it was Kellie out there. "Okay, but let me carry you."

"C-carry me?" Her green eyes widened to twice their size.

"That's what I said." He unlatched the chain, then scooped her into his arms. Ignoring her little squeak, he pushed the gate open with his hip and made long strides through the grass and wildflowers.

As they neared the clearing beneath the tree house, Mark made out the still form his dog sat guarding. He set Holly on her feet, and they both rushed over.

Holly knelt beside her son and eased his head into her lap. "Davey? Honey, it's Mom."

Dirt-encrusted saliva streaked the boy's cheek. He released a soft moan but didn't open his eyes.

"He must have had a seizure," she choked out.

Nodding, Mark slipped in beside Shadow. He could well imagine her distress and was grateful that Shadow had been looking out for the boy. "We should check for injuries." When Holly gave him the go-ahead, he gently palpated Davey's limp body. "A few scratches on his arms and legs, but I'm not finding anything else."

The boy's chest heaved in a deep inhalation. His eyelids fluttered. "M-mom?"

"I'm here, baby. I'm right here." Swallowing a sob, she smoothed back his sweat-matted hair. "How are you feeling?"

"Tired. My head hurts." He shifted his gaze to Mark. "Hi."

"Hi, buddy." Mark shot him a relieved grin, but his voice shook as he asked, "What were you thinking, scaring your mom like this? Scaring all of us?"

Davey scrunched his eyebrows together. "I was mad at you." He sat up and scooted away from his mother. "Mad at both of you."

Holly reached out to him. "We can talk about this later, honey. I should take you home and call Dr. Liggett."

"I don't need to go to the doctor again. Shadow warned me a seizure was coming, so I got safe on the ground first." Shadow had crept into Davey's lap. He wrapped his arms around the dog's neck and buried his face in his fur, as if doing so could hide the tears he obviously didn't want Mark and Holly to see. "I'm sorry for messing up your open house thing, Mom, but I'm okay now. You should go back and do…whatever."

A stricken look contorted her face. "None of that matters now. All I want—all I've *ever* wanted—is for you to be happy and secure."

Ignoring her, Davey hugged Shadow tighter.

"Holly," Mark quietly urged, "go do what you need to do and leave him with me for now. Maybe I can help clear up a few things."

She glanced hesitantly from Mark to her son. "Would you be okay with that, Davey?"

He gave a half-hearted shrug. "If it means I don't have to sit by myself in that stupid conference room."

Studying her son, she worried her lower lip between her teeth. "All right, then," she said at last. She narrowed one eye at Mark. "But you are *not* carrying me back to your truck."

Recalling the feel of her in his arms, he decided those might be the most disheartening words he'd heard yet today.

Holly hoped returning for the open house wasn't a mistake. Davey seemed to be recovering normally from the seizure, but he'd given her one too many scares lately.

When they reached the truck, she climbed into the rear seat with her son and had him stretch out with his head on her lap. Only then did she notice the stains smudging her capris and the dirt and grassy stubble marring the new sandals she'd bought especially for the grand opening.

She needed to let her friends know they'd found Davey, so she called Joella. "Mark's going to look after him, and I'm on my way back. Except my shoes and pants are ruined. Any chance I could borrow something from your closet?"

"Oh, honey, anything you need! Samuel's at the apartment with Sophie. I'll let him know to expect you."

At the barn, Mark waited in the truck with Davey while Holly ran upstairs to change. She chose mint-green slacks that coordinated with her blouse, then slipped her feet into a pair of beige espadrilles. Good thing she and Joella were close enough in size.

With less than an hour before guests would begin to arrive, Mark parked in front of the event center. He shifted to cast Holly an encouraging smile. "Don't worry about a thing. We'll hang out for a bit, have some lunch, and if Davey's feeling up to it in a few hours, I'll bring him over before the festivities wrap up."

"Thank you, Mark. Thank you so much." She turned to Davey, now sitting up next to her with Shadow on his other side. "I love you, sweetie. You know that, right?"

He nodded, his eyelids drooping. "I'm real sorry for scaring you, Mom."

"I know. We'll talk more later." She kissed his forehead, then told Mark, "Make sure he takes it easy."

At his thumbs-up, she reluctantly stepped from the truck, then waved as they drove away. After such a tumultuous morning, how would she ever shift out of terrified-mom mode and mentally gear up for hostess and catering duties?

And Mark! What would she have done if he hadn't rushed back to help? If he hadn't known right where to look for Davey? A shudder coursed through her. She honestly didn't know what might have happened if he hadn't been there for her son...if he hadn't been there for *her*.

You love him, Holly. Why do you keep fighting it?

Only one reason—fear.

But unlike Lindsey, who had once feared her love for Spencer would be forever eclipsed by the Navarro-McClement feud, and Joella, who'd resisted her feelings for Samuel because of her fear of developing Alzheimer's, Holly was afraid of having yet another dream snatched from her grasping fingers. She'd lost her husband, her unborn child, her dreams for the future they should have shared. And today, she'd come so very close to losing the little boy who was her life.

Dare she risk her heart one more time?

Running on autopilot, she somehow made it through the afternoon. The steady flow of guests kept her busy replenishing the buffet tables and responding to inquiries about the catering options River Bend Events offered. When at last the crowd thinned, she looked up from gathering discarded drink cups to see Mark and Davey coming her way. Shadow trotted alongside them, and since he sported an official service dog vest, no one could complain about a dog on the premises.

She dropped the cups in the nearest trash receptacle and hurried over. "How are you feeling, honey? Better?"

"Yeah. A lot." Did her son just look up at Mark and *wink*? "Got any cookies left?" He and Shadow started for the buffet table.

"Don't overdo," she called after him, already knowing her admonition was useless.

"He'll be fine," Mark said. "I fed him a healthy lunch.

High protein, low carb, some fruit and a big glass of milk. Oh, and he had a two-hour nap."

"How can I ever thank you?" *How can I keep my heart from beating out of my chest?*

"No thanks necessary." His gaze held hers. "In case you haven't realized it yet, I'm smitten with y—" He made a choking sound in his throat. "With the kid. Smitten with the kid. Totally."

She glanced around to make sure she wasn't needed anywhere. Only a few guests remained, and it appeared Joella and Lindsey had everything under control. "So," she began, "Davey seems in good spirits. Did you two talk?"

"We did. All good." His voice came out raspy. Covering a discreet cough, he gestured toward a beverage station. "Mind if I get something to drink?"

"Help yourself." She followed him over. "You're not catching anything, I hope?"

"No, I'm, ah— It's just—" He chugged an entire cup of cranberry-orange punch, then plopped down the cup and faced her. "The truth is, I need to tell you something, but figuring out how to say it is making me a nervous wreck."

She clutched her stomach. "Did something else happen with Davey?"

"No, but—"

Davey appeared out of nowhere and poked him in the ribs. "Just tell her, Mark."

"Cool it. I'm trying." Gaze darting, he gripped her hands and tugged her through the door into the rear hallway.

She stumbled and jerked free. "Mark! What's going on?"

"Sorry, I wanted some privacy." With a grating sigh,

he leaned against the opposite wall. "Holly, I'm in love with you. I know I've given you zero reasons to love me back—and a million reasons not to—but there it is. Say the word and I'll never—"

"I'm in love with you, too." She barely heard her own voice over the pounding of her pulse.

He gaped. "Wh-what did you say?"

"I didn't want to fall for you, because you can be *so* exasperating, and I've tried a million times to talk myself out of it…" Head shaking, she stepped closer and palmed his cheek. "But maybe that's exactly why it happened. Because as annoyed as you make me sometimes, I always know your heart's in the right place. I always know you care."

"I do," he rasped, covering her hand with his own. "I care about you so much that it hurts, and if you don't let me kiss you right now—"

She stretched up to silence him with a kiss of her own, and when their lips met, her knees would have given way if he hadn't caught her in his strong arms.

Behind her, cheers and applause rang out. Gasping, she swiveled to see Joella, Lindsey, Davey and several others crowded around the doorway.

Davey pushed through and ran up to her, wrapping one skinny arm around her waist and the other around Mark. He looked up at him with a grin. "See? I told you it'd be okay."

"Yeah, you sure did." Mark tousled the boy's hair.

When Shadow yipped and inserted himself into their group hug, Holly could do nothing but laugh. "You two—or should I say *three*—must have had quite the conversation this afternoon."

"Let's just say you've raised a wise and *very* persuasive young man. Now, if you'll excuse me…" Gripping

Davey's shoulders, Mark aimed him and Shadow back the way they'd come, then signaled the onlookers to quit gawking and close the door.

Alone with him in the hallway, Holly could scarcely breathe. "Is this really happening?"

"Only if you want it to."

"I do." She shivered. "I do!"

Sweeping her into his arms, Mark gave a breathy chuckle. "Glad you've got those two little words memorized, because I hope you'll be needing them in an official capacity in the very near future."

The future. How long had it been since Holly had allowed herself—*truly* allowed herself—to dream? *This is the day which the Lord hath made; we will rejoice and be glad in it.*

This day, yes, but every day was a new day, created by God and filled with new reasons for rejoicing. How could she not live in anticipation? How could she not hope and dream and plan? And though life could be unpredictable, God was changeless, always there, always merciful, always loving.

As for this wonderful, Godly man standing in front of her...

She nestled close, tilting her face up to his. "Don't you think you should kiss me again?"

"I do." His grin widened. "I do, I do, I do!"

And he did.

Epilogue

One year later

Holly clamped a hand on her fidgeting son's shoulder. "Davey, stop squirming and smile at the camera."

"I can't help it, Mom. I'm all itchy."

"That's what you get for rolling in the grass with Shadow." She'd spent the last five minutes plucking grass and twigs out of her son's hair and the dog's coat so they'd be presentable for the picture. She couldn't complain, though. Davey had thrived this past year. His seizures were fewer and farther between, and he'd made the honor roll almost every grading period.

The photographer, perched on a stepladder outside the Hands and Heart Nature Preserve entrance, waved his cap to get their attention. "Okay, we're almost ready. I just need the couple on the end to squeeze in a bit closer."

"Sorry," Lindsey called, "but with this pregnant belly, I'm about as squeezed as I can get."

Snuggled close to Holly on a wrought-iron bench, Mark reached his arm around her slightly expanded waistline and whispered, "That'll be you in a few months."

She laughed as his breath tickled her ear. "Stop! You're going to ruin the picture."

Could she be any happier? This had been a year filled with more blessings than she could have imagined. First, her marriage to Mark last summer, right here among friends and family in the newly established preserve. They'd lived in Holly's apartment while Mark built an Austin-stone house for them next door to Samuel and Joella. The updated cabin, which Alicia had deeded to Mark, was now used as an overnight rental for honeymooning River Bend Events clients.

In the meantime, Holly had been approached by Bonnie Stanley from the bistro with a proposition. Bonnie had heard—Holly never did find out from whom, but she had her suspicions—about her dream of opening a tearoom. Bonnie had wanted for a long time to expand her business to include a separate bakery, and since the shop space on Central remained vacant, what if they leased it jointly?

Together they'd drawn up a new business plan and worked through partnership legalities with an attorney. Based on Bonnie's sterling reputation plus the ongoing success of River Bend Events, the bank had taken no time at all to approve a start-up loan. The Forget-Me-Not Café and Bonnie's Bakery had opened last September to rave reviews.

So far, Holly had successfully divided her time between the café and River Bend Events. That could all change once this new baby came along, but if the past couple of years had taught her anything, it was that God could always be counted on—even, and sometimes *especially*, when things didn't go exactly as hoped.

She only had to look into the eyes of her husband and son to know this was true.

* * *

"One more," the photographer called. "Everybody look up here and say, 'I love my family!'"

Family. Never in a million years could Mark have imagined how significant that little word would become. All those years of wishing for a sibling or two, wondering why his mother had all but cut ties with her Texas roots, hoping Rae would change her mind about having more kids...

And then they'd lost Kellie, the only child Mark had thought he'd ever have.

Now, today, as they celebrated the one-year anniversary of Hands and Heart Nature Preserve, he looked around at this big, beautiful family arrayed beside and behind him.

Mom and Dad, who'd flown down from Missoula especially for this day. Holly's mother, holding a framed portrait of Holly's dad, who'd passed away last winter. Uncle Hank, Aunt Lois and Aunt Audra. Samuel, Joella and little Sophie. Spencer and Lindsey, expecting their first child in a couple of weeks, along with Lindsey's mother and stepdad from Florida.

Even Mark's biological father, Owen McClement, had made a point of coming. They'd gradually been getting to know each other, and with understanding came forgiveness and healing—for Mark as well as for his mother and Lindsey.

Best of all, right beside him sat the woman who, along with her amazing son, had truly made his life complete. Holly's love had sanded off his rough edges, taught him how to trust God again, made him want to be the best husband and father possible. Every time he looked into those gorgeous green eyes, he loved her more.

"That should do it." The photographer climbed down

and stowed his camera in its case. "I'll email a link in a few days so you can view the proofs and order any prints you'd like."

Mark stood and shook his hand. "Thanks for being so patient with this mob. Can you stay and join us for the barbecue?" The aromas from Hank's smoker had been teasing his taste buds for the past hour.

"Wish I could, but thanks to all the business River Bend Events has sent my way, I'm booked for a wedding in Georgetown this evening and need to get going."

The photographer left, and the family dispersed to arrange folding tables and set out the food. Soon they were dining on Hank's brisket and sausage, Lois's spicy baked beans, and Holly's creamy mac and cheese. Hefty servings of pecan and blueberry pies from Bonnie's Bakery topped off a meal sure to pack on a few extra pounds around Mark's middle.

Later, he took Holly's hand and drew her to the riverbank, where they could watch the sun slip behind purple hills. He tucked her head against his shoulder and sighed. "I never thought I'd be this happy again. Never thought I deserved to be."

"Good thing God doesn't give us what we deserve, because otherwise I wouldn't have you. Or Davey." Voice cracking, she laid a hand on her abdomen. "Or the hope of this new life growing inside me."

"Our baby," he murmured, his eyes filling. "For as long as I live, I will never stop thanking God for bringing me to Texas…for bringing me home to *you*."

* * * * *

Dear Reader,

I'm especially fond of this final installment of The Ranchers of Gabriel Bend. It has taken three books for the characters, each on journeys of discovery and growth, to put the effects of the Navarro-McClement feud behind them. That isn't unlike our real-world struggles. It can sometimes take months, years or even decades to grapple with past hurts and to forge a better future.

There will be times, though, when setbacks erase whatever progress we thought we'd made, and it'll feel like starting from scratch. But that doesn't mean our efforts are futile. God can help us grow stronger through each trial as He teaches us something about ourselves and about His eternal love, if only we remain receptive. Stay hopeful and faithful, my friends. God is with you!

Thank you for spending time with me in fictional Gabriel Bend, Texas. I love hearing from my readers, so please contact me through my website, www.MyraJohnson.com, where you can also subscribe to my e-newsletter.

With prayers and gratitude,
Myra

LOVE INSPIRED

Stories to uplift and inspire

Fall in love with Love Inspired—
inspirational and uplifting stories of faith
and hope. Find strength and comfort in
the bonds of friendship and community.
Revel in the warmth of possibility and the
promise of new beginnings.

Sign up for the Love Inspired newsletter
at **LoveInspired.com** to be the first
to find out about upcoming titles,
special promotions and exclusive content.

CONNECT WITH US AT:

 Facebook.com/LoveInspiredBooks

Twitter.com/LoveInspiredBks

What are you thinking?

Apparently, she wasn't. Jalissa straightened her shoulders and slipped her mental armor on. Just because Rider had been perfectly charming with her family didn't mean she'd let that soften her toward him. He was still arrogant, immature and a touch reckless.

"Morning, Tucker," Rider said when he opened her door. "Captain Simms's wife is already here and has set up the perfect spot for the shoot." Rider pointed toward the rear of the van. "Animals in the back?"

"Yes. They're all in crates."

He opened the back doors then shook his head. "How did you survive the ride with all that noise?"

"Found my happy place." And one day she'd see Hawaii in person. She loosened Flo and moved back so the dog could exit the van through the driver's side.

"You know what happiness is?" Rider smirked.

"Hardy har-har." Jalissa rounded the back to start unloading the animals. "Where am I putting them?"

"Oh, don't worry about it." Rider cupped his mouth. "Young, Trent, Barns, come help!"

She wiggled a finger in her eardrum. "I think your voice carries well enough without you shouting."

"Maybe, but I have no idea where they are in the firehouse. Now you don't have to carry the animals. Plus, the guys already know where everything is set up."

"Then I can leave?" She had a load of laundry she could do.

"Oh, no." He tsked at her. "We need your assistance with the animals."

Jalissa slowly inched backward but stopped when Flo nudged her. *One…two…* She could do this. Be near the firehouse for help. She didn't actually have to go *inside*, did she? Flo licked her fingertips.

"All right," Jalissa said slowly. "I'll just stay out of everyone's way unless I'm needed."

"You'll be needed." He stared into her eyes.

She blinked slowly. What was going on with her? First thinking Rider was good-looking, and now they were having some kind of moment. She needed to fix this real quick. "I'm sure. It's not like I can trust you to be competent."

The firemen rounded the back of the van, ignoring her conversation with Rider. They quietly began unloading the crates.

Rider rocked back on his heels, sliding his hands into his pockets. "Shots fired in, what?" He pulled an arm up to glance at his watch. "Five minutes. Must be some kind of record for you."

"Whatever." She gave him a wide berth and followed the last fireman from the side parking lot to the front of the firehouse.

She inhaled. *One…two…three…four…* Exhale. *Five…six… seven…eight…* Flo bumped into her hand as if to let Jalissa know she wasn't alone. She buried her fingers in the soft fur as they strolled up the walkway.

Don't miss
An Unlikely Alliance *by Toni Shiloh,*
available July 2022
wherever Love Inspired books and ebooks are sold.

LoveInspired.com

LIEXP0522